T. HEARTLESS

Dave & Treasure: A Chicago Love Story

First edition

This book was professionally typeset on Reedsy.
Find out more at reedsy.com

Contents

Prologue

Sounds of screeching tires awake Treasure from her nap. Adjusting her eyes from the bright sun, she screamed in terror. She gives direct eye contact to the driver on the side of them. Noticing the familiar face, that turned out to be Trenell. Treasure crazy ex-

boyfriend has been following us. He picked the wrong time to appear in her life. Damn near knocking them off the road, all she could hear was Dave yelling, "Hold on." Taking a sharp left to avoid a collision he goes down a one-way street. Dave pulled over immediately.

"Are you okay, do you have a clue of who that was? I have noticed this same vehicle sitting in random places before," Turning to Treasure looking for an answer.

"I'm not sure, but from what I was able to see of him, it looked like my ex Trenell," She responds, holding her head down in disbelief.

"I'm not mad at you for defending us, Dave not at all, trust me if I knew he was out, I would have mentioned it," Treasure response.

"Well, you're not leaving me, now that I know this lunatic is out and trying to harm you and our child. What kind of man would I be if I allowed him the chance to even come as close as he just did to harm you? With me right at your side, we have to get you some protection," I said.

This entire situation has caused me to get out of character and turn into the hood, overprotective me again. I couldn't believe what I had gotten involved in. I refuse to allow it to take over my happiness. With this happening, there is no way I would allow her to stay at her place by herself. Treasure sat in the passenger seat, looking hurt and confused. I didn't understand why, but I was going to find out what was bothering her.

"Are you okay? I hope so," I ask her.

"Yes, I'm okay, Hun. I'm just trying to figure out how long and when did he get out," she utters, giving of a blank stare out the window.

"It's okay. We're still going out to celebrate that shit is not about to destroy this moment of happiness between us. We will worry about that later," I assured her.

We had just left the doctor's appointment, and it's true, Treasure was indeed ten weeks pregnant. And now I was more than excited to make her mine forever, with our little blessing on the way.

"Dave, can we just do something in the house, I don't want to go out tonight. Just us two celebrating at home?"

"Sure, love it's whatever you want to do. Let's stop at the grocery store to get a few items, and then we can head to our place.

"Our place, don't you mean your place."

"No, I mean our place. You will not be staying by yourself anymore. Not, with that psycho out there on the loose and especially with you being the mother of my child nope not in this ballpark," I reached for her hand , kissed it and smiled.

"Okay, Mister, I like how you jumped right into decision making, but I can't just leave my home like that."

"It's okay I got you don't worry about it, I will make sure everything is just fine," I said.

Making it to the grocery store, I reach over to the glove department and grabbed my gun, gripping the holster and putting it on my hip before we exit. Treasure looked at me with this look of shock while licking her lips.

"Oh, you're a bad boy in disguise, I see. I knew it was in you?" Laughing and waiting for me to help her out the car.

"Come on, lady, let's go," I reply while reaching for her hand. Heading into the grocery store, Treasure started picking up items she would want to eat.

"So, we're cooking together or on your own," I asked her.

"Great suggestion, it will be fun together, I'll assist, and you take over," She replied.

Grabbing her from behind and kissing her neck I whisper in her hear, "Okay, it's a deal as long as I can have you for dessert," I smiled and smacked her ass while grabbing a can of whip cream.

"See, that's how we end up with this little bundle of joy now you can't keep your hands off me," Treasure laughed.

"I can't help it. I love to give my woman attention, so she has no reason to seek it elsewhere," I reply.

"I love every bit of it, especially the public affection," Treasure response.

Continuing with our little grocery shopping. We get everything required for our little celebration dinner. The trip home was quick. Treasure falls asleep, I look over at her just not believing that she is now baring my child. Knowing that I will protect her in every way, without a doubt.

One

Your Mine

A guy like me goes for what he wants, and usually get what he wants. This is what I kept telling myself leaving Starbucks one morning. I kept telling myself she was mine forever, when I ran into her. I noticed that the workers would have conversations with her, so I figured she must be one of their regulars. I watched her for two days straight every morning as she came out of Starbucks. Not being a creep or anything, while getting my daily cup of coffee. Finding the courage to approach her, I decided today was the day I finally took the bait.

She stood to be about five feet five inches with a nice fat ass, small waist, and she was always well dressed. Sitting in Starbucks I waited for her to walk in. As she walked to the register to pay, I swipe my card to process her payment. From the look on her face, she doesn't look grateful by my actions. Not knowing what to expect, she mouths aloud. "Slow down, man. I appreciate you paying, but do I know you."

Snickering at her and giving her this look of amazement, I whisper in her ear, "Let's get to know each other then, why don't we."

To my surprise, she reacted with a smile, "Sure, why not, I'm not in a rush."

Grabbing my order and walking over towards the condiment section for the cream, sugar, and cinnamon, I waited for her. Watching her make her coffee and taking a mental note of how she prepares her coffee. I suggest that she find a seat.

"Well, my name is Davion people call me Dave for short. I work in a factory overnight as a fork-lifter. Not only that, but I am a successful business owner. I have a bachelor's degree in Business Administrations with a minor in Accounting. Born and raised here in Chicago, no kids and I never been married. What else did I miss?" Showing off my pearly whites I smiled. "Tell me about yourself, Ms. lady?"

"Wow!! Deep well, my name is Treasure. I work for a law firm been there for a few years. I'm pursuing my Masters in English, and I have my Bachelor's in Criminal Justice. I currently work as a Paralegal. I paid my way through college to avoid loans and stayed at home with my parents until I finished. Now I stay in a two-bedroom condo and drive a Monte Carlos, and I also never been married," she sighed with relief after responding.

"Wow, you are impressive, you're one of a kind, paying your way through school out of pocket without student loans takes a lot of determination. Determine, a beauty and intelligent woman I see. Can I take you out on a date later tonight? I don't want to keep you waiting, after all you look like your heading to the gym.

She scratched her head, and stuttered, "Sure, why don't we, and yes I am," she stated.

Pulling my phone out my pocket to exchange numbers, I explained to her, "Not to cut our conversation short or anything, but I have a meeting that I need to attend," I disclosed.

"My bad, I don't want to keep you waiting, but okay here is my number, by the way," she said.

Pulling out her Galaxy and inserting my number, we depart, with a brief hug. I immediately text her, to be ready at 7:00 pm. Which she texted back her address *6126 Ravens-wood Avenue.*

Walking out of Starbucks, noticing the time. "Damn it," I yell.

Running late to my meeting, I send Candice a text to see if she has started.

Me: Hey, Candice have you started the meeting?

Her: Yes, started about fifteen minutes ago.

Me: Thank you! I'm on my way now running a little behind schedule.

On my way to the restaurant, I just couldn't stop thinking about Treasure already. I know people have their flaws especially me. I just need to make sure she was the one for me. So far, I liked what I saw. Everything that looked good on the outside might not be right on the inside. I just had to discover her. Making it to my meeting I discussed the excellent progress the business had been making and to also reward my employees for keeping things running smoothly.

* * *

Arriving to the restaurant and to the conference room with little time to spare.

Walking in I apologize immediately,

"For my tardiness I would like to give you all the weekend off with pay. The only thing I expect is that we all make it to the

catering event an hour early Sunday afternoon to setup. If everyone agree can you raise your hand," I ask.

To my surprise, in unison, everyone agreed.

"With that being said the meeting is complete, please make sure you clock out," Candice announce before everyone depart.

I walk over to Candice, "Thank you for covering the meeting without me. I owe you one because you're always on point with everything," I convey to her.

"So, what have you all relaxed and in a blissful mood? Not saying you're not always relaxed, but it's like you didn't bother to go over the meeting agenda to be sure everything was covered," Candice asks.

"Well, Ms. Candice, I just may have found the one for me. You know the saying a man who finds a woman shall find a wife, I think I have."

"I'm happy for you if you have because you deserve it. Just make sure you stay open and honest to her."

"Well, your right about that. I will most definitely have to be open. The

3

energy between us is unexplainable."

"I pray that she is, and they say if the energy is right, then the connection will be wonderful."

"Yeah that is true. Oh yeah, I will be here tonight for our first date, I need you to play it safe, she doesn't know I'm the owner let the team know. I guess, I'll see you guys later thank you so much Candice," I explain.

"Okay, I'll see you tonight," she responds.

Leaving the restaurant, Treasure come to mind instantly. Honestly, I had enough with searching, and I just prayed after tonight things could go well with me and her. I don't chase women as most men do. So, for me to actual take action how I did to get her attention was out of my character. I just hope it's all worth it.

Taking the drive home, I turned on some R&B soul music, making it through traffic with ease. I stop to grab me some lunch before getting home, *Wing Stop,* it is. I decide not to go gym today, after I having my lunch, I make my way home to get some rest and prepare for the night.

Two

Date Night

I woke up from my cat nap feeling refreshed and anxious...so I texted her;

Me: I hope you aren't flanking out on me and trying to pull a quick one.

Walking through my crib turning on my iPod dock, I hit the playlist for some hood music and chose *Kevin Gates Hard For*. It went well with my mood. Taking a quick shower and walking into my walk-in closet, I reach for my black bomber jacket, Lacoste fitted polo top, and some black fitted jeans. I wasn't trying to over dress so I chose something casual. Calling the restaurant to make sure reservation was setup perfect, which took two minutes to verify. My text alert goes off after hanging up and its Treasure,

Tre: If I wanted to send you off, you wouldn't have my number or address. Should I wear something casually or romantic, don't want to be overly dressed.

Me: Wear whatever you feel is comfortable for you, and okay I see you in a few.

Ding! (text message alert)

Tre: Alright

I like her attitude; she's bold and gets her point across. I justpray she can deal with me even through the hard times. The saying a man who

finds a wife makes a happy life. I believe she is the one
for me, and I just hope we can pull through the hard times together.

Deciding to bring out my Lexus for the event. I enter her address in the GPS, and blast Trey Songs in the background while taking the expressway. Getting through traffic in less than fifteen minutes. I look at the time its ten minutes before seven. Arriving to her house, I park and spray myself with some cologne before getting out.

Oh well, I hope she ready, I thought to myself. I go to ring the bell, and to my surprise there she was looking even more beautiful than this morning. "Hey D, your kind of early. Come in, I just need to grab my clutch," she said, interrupting me from staring. I walked in and sat on her bar stool and noticed she had a wine collection sitting on the top of the island.

"Treasure, do you mind if I pour us a glass of wine before we leave."

"Go ahead, why don't you," she responded. I pour us a glass of *Chardonnay*, just as she come sashaying in front of the island. I hand her a glass and suggest to make a toast, "To new everlasting beginnings of happiness for the both of us throughout this journey of life," I said as we clinked our glasses.

We drank and while downing mine I looked at her and said, "You're gorgeous, even though this morning was the best look for me...all natural," I sarcastically said with a smile.

She smiled and responded, "Oh, why thank you so much, and you looking like a model from a GQ magazine shoot yourself, sexy."

"Let's get up out of here woman before we end up stuck here," I responded. She looks at me and laugh with this enlightening smile spread across her face. I reach for the door waiting for her to exit. She set her alarm system and strolled over to my ride.

The first thing that came out her mouth was, "You must be a very wealthy man to be riding in a Lexus," she states.

"You can pretty much say I am; I have worked my ass off and still do to be able to afford the finer things in life without
worrying. I don't do it to impress anyone. I do it just to make sure my future family and I are okay. Shall I add, you can and will have the finer things in life soon."

That left her speechless I waited for her smart remark, but nothing to my surprise. I opened the door for her, and she reached to close it, I tap her hand, "No, I'm not a man who allows what's soon to be his to close or open a door of any entrance or exit for herself."

She gives me this look of shock and slowly a smile crept across her face. I close the door behind her and hopped in the driver's seat and just smile to myself. Thinking to myself, yes, I'm going to have fun with making her apart of my future.

Turning on the music, we arrive to the restaurant with ten minutes to spare. I help her out the car and toss my keys to the valet, winking my eye and throwing him a tip. Holding her hand as we get to the entrance of the restaurant.

"I always wanted to go to this place but haven't found the time or right person to go with me," She squeals with excitement in her voice.

"Well, I guess you are going to enjoy every moment of being here tonight, because you finally found that person to go with." I reply.

We walk inside side by side, and the waitress sat us in my favorite area of the restaurant. I had no choice but to tip her as well because my team was doing a great job with the role of treating me like a guest. A lot of people didn't know I was the owner. I tend to keep my face out of the public view. It's a pretty upscale private owned restaurant. I'm always doing things for the community, down to fundraising and catering to significant events which keeps the team busy.

Back to my night with, Miss Treasure. I look at her and smile, "So, do you like what you see?" I ask.

She turns to face me and respond, "The owner has some great taste. I love the interior layout and design. Like who would think to put two different themes inside a restaurant, and it turning out to look this great.

I love the whole atmosphere of this place, and the service so far is great." "Silly, I'm talking about me, not this place," I chuckle and respond. "Oh, my fault

The waiter come back to our booth with menus, and my favorite drink in hand.

She gives me this uncertainty look.

Shaking my head, I laugh, "I request for it when I made reservation. You don't have to look like that," I reply in response to her facial expression.

She laughs and sarcastically remark, "I was about to assume you must come here often."

"Is there anything specific you would like to order ma'am," the waitress ask Treasure, directly.

"Yes, *Armand De Brignac Demi-Sec Champagne*," she requests.

"Okay, *Armand Champagne* coming up," the waitress responds and walks off.

"You have a great taste in wine, I see."

"I have a whole collection of fine wine underneath my bar stand at home," she responded.

"So, Miss Treasure, can I ask you something?"

"Go ahead, ask me anything," Treasure replies.

"Alright, so tell me what your previous relationship was like.

Taking a long deep breath in and out, "My last relationship was very toxic," she hesitates to continue.

Cutting her off instantly, "Hold on what you mean when you say toxic like physical, mental abuse toxic?"

"Both," she responds while drifting off into space. "I was just like every other woman who falls in love and find try to make it work," She sighs, leaving this look of disbelief across her face.

I had no choice but to end the questions for her, not wanting to leave her with any regrets tonight.

"Well, my previous relationship was okay. We separated due to her wanting a man to provide her every need. Like she was brilliant and had a career as a nurse, but she didn't want to work. So, we decided to go our separate ways because we just weren't compatible with each other besides in the bedroom. We lasted for about two years. She was missing work, just to get me to pay her bills and to spend my money on her shopping addiction. That took the cake for me, so I changed my locks. I sent her a farewell gift and told her I couldn't deal with her anymore. She mailed my old set of keys to me in the mail and that was the end for us" I mention.

Tre look at me and shake her head, "So you sent her a farewell gift ending your relationship that easily, wow. I guess you guys both felt it would end soon for it to end so well."

"I guess we did. I understand now why you're surprised by my actions," I add.

* * *

The waitress come back to give her the drink she requests and see if we're ready to order.

"Not quite yet, I'm still looking over the menu," Tre reply.

"Okay, I will be back in about five minutes is that okay with you? She replies before walking off.

Focusing back to Treasure, with her drink in hand she takes a sip and states, "So you're quite a gentleman, is it to all women you meet or just me."

"This is my true character to everyone," I assure her. Picking up the drink and pouring myself another shot. "How long did this toxic relationship last?

Treasure gulp down the last of her drink and replied, "Three long years."

"Oh, wow long time, do you have any other questions for me," I insist.

"I sure do, but I will wait. I have a list in my head," She laughs.

I laugh at her sarcasm. Finding out more in detail about her, makes me more intrigue with her.

Treasure ordered Crab legs with sautéed shrimp meal. I request for the T-Bone Steak with sautéed shrimp on the side dinner. Candice, repeat the orders and asked if we would want any appetizer. We both decline and she leave.

Treasure instantly went in for the kill with the questions, "So, what is it you look for in a woman? What turns you on & off? Somethings you like to do during your spare time with your mate?"

Bursting out in laughter, "Well you are the type of woman I want. I like everything about you." Treasure blushes.

"What turns me on as far as a woman well it's obvious, got to be a hard worker, strong, have goals, family-oriented, and most of all someone who wants to make her life better with or without me. As far as looks beauty can be found on both the inside and outside, so if she can't define beauty within herself, she as a woman needs to reevaluate her life. I don't care if it's your eyes, lips, the arch in your walk, it's the simple things. I know women are the happiest when their hair and nails are done. I don't mind making sure to keep those little tasks paid for or scheduled for her. A happy woman makes a happy life, for both the man she's with and her family. So, from there, you can figure out my turnoffs. I love an open-minded, self spoken woman because if you are willing to discuss anything with me, I know your willing to talk when things aren't right. I don't ask for a lot because I want to be able to give those same attributes." I respond.

Grabbing my drink, I toss the last of it down. Looking over to Treasure she was sitting with a smile across her face with all her pearly whites showing.

"So, I can't complain, man, your very particular about what you want, and that's fine with me," she responds.

The crew walks over with our food in hand and place our meals on the table with ease. I grabbed my napkin and put it on my lap, Treasure clears her throat and ask, "Do you mind if we pray?"

"Of course, go right ahead," I express to her. I didn't expect her to ask that. This brings out an even more attractive side in her after hearing that. Being spiritual wasn't something I expected from her. She prayed over our meals, and both respond with an Amen. Thinking to myself, *A woman who believed in prayer, I must get to know her and find out more about her.*

"So, do you go to church every Sunday. Do you have a religion? I hope I'm not offending you. I just would like to know," I asked.

"Well, I'm glad you asked instead of assuming. I am not a churchgoing woman at all. I don't believe you have to go to church every Sunday to pray. I'm not religious. I just pray for better days and life accomplishments. I meditate and pray to keep my life afloat for greatness. After being in an abusive relationship, I go about life in a different way," She confirms.

I had no words for her after that response. Thinking to myself, *she is the woman for me. I genuinely believe in my heart she is mine forever, and I will do whatever it is to keep her. She is everything I could ask for in a woman. She is not with me for my money, hopefully, not for my looks.*

Treasure disturbs my thoughts and shoots me with more questions.

"What is it that your looking forward to tonight, after this date?" She asks.

Catching me off guard, I didn't think she would ask such a question.

"Well, um uh," Clearing my throat I continued. "Well Treasure, if you don't mind me calling you Tre, I plan to keep in touch with you and hopefully we can grow and build a relationship. I don't want sex, that's the last thing I expect on the first night out. I want to get to know you honestly speaking. I have been coming to Starbucks daily, after we bumped into each other. I told myself, you we're the one for me. I just hoped you found me just as attractive as I did you and not take me as a fool or as a stalker. I am far from both those characteristics. I just was taught as a man if you want something you have to go out and get it," I express.

Treasure stared into my eyes, and this massive smile with this sparkle in her eyes came out of nowhere. I instantly caught this warm feeling in my heart and reached to grab her hand. I kissed it, and

whispered to her, "I promise I don't want to hurt you."

She looks at me and responds, "I will believe it as we progress."

"I am a man of my words and promise to make you the happiest woman ever, and you won't regret it."

Tre laughs while grabbing a crab leg, and begin to eat. I was enjoying myself already with her, and she didn't even know it. Picking up my knife and fork to cut my steak, I noticed she was looking at me and blurted out in laughter, "I hope you're not embarrassed because I don't like using the crab leg utensil to crack my crabs. It's time-consuming if you ask me. I do have manners I just don't like using the utensil," she mentions.

I had no choice but to laugh and decide to excuse myself from the table. I asked Tony, the valet for tonight, to drive my car to my house for me because, I plan to enjoy my night with her. As requested, he did exactly just that and sent me a picture to show me. I request for a Lyft ride to get him back here to work. I had to enjoy my night with my future and not worry about being the driver. I decided to head to the bar and request a bottle of the drink she order to our table.

"Hey, Candice can you bring me a personal bottle of Armand De Brignac Demi-Sec Champagne please?" I asked.

"Right after I serve these guests," she replies.

On my way back to the table, Treasure wasn't looking, she had this worried look on her face. I had to ask her what the cause of her anxious facial expression. "Oh, nothing just was thinking about a past issue," she answered.

"Oh, okay, stop thinking of the past and let's focus on the future," I reply.

She smiles and proceeds to eat the last of her crab legs.

"So, Treasure, I would love to know more about you like the basic what is your favorite color, birthday, food, and more. I can guess your favorite color is it peach and silver."

She looked at me and replied, "How you figure that?"

"Just know a man pays attention to how a woman decorates certain parts of their home. Like for example, their bathroom, bedroom, and kitchen, I couldn't see two out of those three rooms," I respond.

Before I could continue, Candice came with the bottle resting in a bucket of ice. I poured Treasure and myself another cup.

She looked at me and said, "AWWWWWW, you pay attention. I like that in a man. There is no way I could ever allow myself to let you just drift away from me so quickly.

"A man who is interested in a woman should always pay attention to a lot of things about her without having to ask basic questions when it's obvious," I declared. "See Treasure, what I learned from my mother as a child, was that women would give you answers to all your basic questions right before your eyes if you pay attention. I know you're probably like this is just the beginning of us, but I see just from being here with you for over an hour that your mine. You are the other half of my life," I verbalized.

With that, she reached for her drink and tossed it back with two gulps. "I hope I'm not moving too fast for having these thoughts about you," I respond.

She smiled and said, "No, so far, you're everything a woman could ask for in a man."

"Now, don't make your decision so soon, we have a few more dates to go on before making that judgment," I said.

"Oh, how you know I would accept your few more dates, mister." she stated.

"Well, Treasure, can I finish getting to know you as a person. I would like to know what your favorite things to do and your favorite place to spend quality time. Not just to take you out, but to learn you as a person. If you don't mind before we check out, are you trying to be home at a specific time tonight?" I asked.

"No, I don't have work in the morning, do you have something else planned?" She asked.

"Alright, if you're up to it, I would like to take you to one of my favorite places to relax and breathe," I replied.

Candice, came back to the table and asked if we were ready for the bill.

"Yes, just give us a few to finish up the last of our meal," I responded. Treasure had devoured everything on her plate and even requested for a take-out order of crab legs. I looked up and smiled before asking if she was ready to check out. She nodded her head, yes. I got Candice's attention and she brought the bill and handed it to me while taking our plates to clean the table. I slide my black card inside the checkbook, sign the receipt, and left her with a generous tip for the night. My second family, as I called my employees did a great job with everything.

Treasure and I exited the restaurant and I waved down the first cab that came our way. Giving the driver the address to our destination, I looked over towards Treasure and asked, "So I can assume you enjoyed your meal tonight?

"Yes, I surely did which is the reason I ordered to go, "she laughed.

"So, if I have to guess crab legs is your favorite seafood," I implied.

Treasure looked surprise but gave me direct eye contact and stated, "You have the most beautiful bedroom eyes, and yes, it is."

I grab Treasure's hand and looked at her eye to eye for the very first time tonight and notice this gaze of light in them that glowed. It sent me into a warm feeling. Reaching for her face I kissed her gently. She responds by opening her mouth and allowing our tongues to intertwine. To my surprise, the kiss didn't make me feel nervous or anything. It felt welcoming. I remove my lips from hers and whispered, "Thank you."

The driver pulled up to the giving destination while she gazed out the window. I paid for the ride and reached for her hand after I exited. She got out of the car, and we walked over to the dock and had a seat. She looked up at the stars and grab my hand and said, "What a relaxing moment."

We used the alone time to get to know each other better and found out, we had a lot more in common than we thought. She loved coming to the beach to paint and sip. It's her way of relaxing. I went there to get a piece of mind and do whatever business work I need to get out the way. It's kind of odd because we both have empty homes that we can find several places to relax, but we both prefer outdoor relaxing.

She opened up to me and told me she hadn't always been an open-minded person. Her last relationship had taught her a lot of things and changed a lot about her in both good and bad ways. I let her know she would never have to worry about me putting my hands on her for anything if it isn't to please her both physically and mentally. I hate that she has been through the storm of being with a disrespectful man, but I love it because of the new characteristics that she had which was appealing to me.

She asked, "Do you have any brothers or sisters."

"Yes, I have a brother, no sisters. He is in college pursuing his Ph.D. to become a Neurologists; he has a Master's in Psychology," I tell her. I find out she was the only child and had no siblings. We end the night off right before it started pouring down. I place in a request for a Lyft to drop her off home first. We don't do much talking on the way to her house. She drifts off to sleep. We reach her place, and I help her out and walked her to the door. We share a goodnight kiss, and she looked up saying,

Walking back to the Lyft driver, I smile even harder. I finally got the woman I been searching for. God is good. All while dancing to the car. The Lyft driver looked at me and said, "You guys make a great couple." "Thank you, but it's just our first date out," I

respond

Lost in my thoughts on the way home, just thinking about her. I can say I enjoyed myself tonight for this to be our first date we really did get off on a good start. To me impromptu dates turn out to be the best, so I didn't bother to plan. I did want to plan a trip to Jamaica for us after making it official between us in due time. The driver pulled up to my home and my car was parked right where I expected. The night left me feeling hopeful coming home after enjoying myself with someone other than my homies. I took a shower before ending my night.

Treasure

Watching him out the blinds, I laughed. This man is just gorgeous and perfect. I can't believe he danced his way to the car. I video called my best friend Starr, I had to tell her about tonight. She had to do the most, though, because I didn't tell her about him before the date. Her ass was so dramatic, I just brushed it off. The first thing that came out of her mouth after telling her I went on a date is if he has a brother.

Starr and I grew up, as adults together we attended the same college. She was going for her B.A in Business Administrations and Accounting. We walked across the stage right behind each other. She ended up finding out she was pregnant two weeks before graduation and I became the Godmother to her daughter, whom she named Trinity. So, we weren't just best friends; we were more like sisters. Everything about me, she knew. The woman could write a book about my life story as if it was her life, that's how close we became during college and after.

Continuing are conversation, "Girl, his brother doesn't want you.

"Look here; I'm tired of you picking up these gentlemen and aren't checking out their bros for me," Starr states.

Starr is crazy people say we are like night & day. She helps me get through a lot in life. "I'm going to find a Mr. Right for you and a great father figure to my God baby." "So, where did you go, bitch, spill the tea, "She began to go off.

Fixing my usual cup of tea, I placed my iPad on the countertop, filling my teapot up with cold water to brew my tea before I start talking.

"Well, he bumped into me today, at Starbucks down the street from my place. I saw him before walking out one morning," I responded...

"So, you telling me you saw him before and didn't get his number bitch, are you tripping?" Star rude ass interrupted me.

"Okay, rudeness, but I glanced at him and noticed he was handsome. Don't act like you don't know me. See today was different; he not only bumped into me, but he paid for my shit before I could even get in the store. So, I'm guessing just like I saw him the other day, he saw me as well," I tell her.

"Oh, okay, you lucky bitch, what he looks like," Starr asks. She so noisy and wants to know every detail. "Well, he has these beautiful bedroom light brown eyes that caught my attention immediately," I respond.

"Don't tell me he a light skin ass nigga," she asks. I damn near spilled my tea laughing at her stupid ass,

"No, he chocolate and stands about 6'5, with a muscular build. He has great taste in clothes and has a sharp eye for details," I tell her.

"Girl, I hope his brother looks just as good," She responds.

"Can you stop with your charade of foolishness child. Anyhow, what has my little Goddess been up to? I'm going to come get her for the weekend and take her out," I said, changing the subject.

"My little gem is doing wonderful she loves school and has been asking about you today," She responds.

"Anyhow back to you and mystery man, sister," Starr dramatically replied.

"He is a real gentleman; I can tell you that. I have work in the am, so I will call you while I'm on my way," I interrupted her. Using the time to end the conversation, before we disconnect. I then began prepared myself for bed like I always did. I let my candles in my dining room and turned my music on to my favorite R&B slow songs. Heading to the bathroom, I put on my face cream and got in the shower allowing the water to soothe me. It's my way of meditating every night. I got out, grabbed my robe, and poured myself one last cup of tea. I found myself sitting in the front room, just embracing the calm feeling while trying not to allow my past to get the best of me, after trying this dating thing again. Not a day goes by that I didn't think of my baby girl.

I start to meditate, fresh air one, two, three, four, five counting to ten and breathing. I tend to overthink and let it get the best of me. So far, Dave seems like a good man with great charisma. Let me see if he made it home. I text him goodnight and ask if he made it home. He texted back.

Dave: *Oh my gosh, I totally forgot yes sweetie, and goodnight, see you soon.*

I blushed after reading his texts. I went to brush my teeth for the night and grabbed myself a cold bottle of water, before placing it on my nightstand for the middle of the night. I drifted off to sleep with ease soon as my head touched my pillow.

Three

Great Vibes

Sleeping like a baby and, to my surprise, waking up twenty minutes before my alarm went off. I felt refreshed, so I brewed myself a cup of tea like I did every morning, and blended myself a fruit smoothie. I grabbed my snack of oatmeal for work and placed it

in my lunch bag. I then went to take care of my morning hygiene and prepared for work. I didn't even hear my text message notification go off before getting in the shower, but to my surprise, my phone was blowing up. If I could recall, it went off at least six times before I got in the shower. I looked to see who it was, and it was both Starr and Dave. Dave's message reads:

"Good Morning sweetie, I had you on my mind all night before drifting off to sleep. Have a good day at work today and remember there is someone who loves the person you are". He followed it with a with GIF of a painted portrait of a man & woman relaxing on the beach.

I replied with a good morning and how thoughtful of you.

Starr texted me her usually good morning, a picture of my God Baby, and a request to meet each other for lunch since we worked down the street from each other. I love my bestie; we are more like sisters from another mother.

She keeps me on my toes as far as everything, and I do the same for her. I sent her some money for my God baby through the cash app and tell her to get my baby whatever it is she want for breakfast this morning. She hated it when I did this, but she loved it because it helps her in a way to not cook in the morning, which gives them more time to get ready.

Leaving out, I locked up and set my alarm before grabbing my things. I smiled on my way to my car for no reason in mind. While on my way out the door, I notice a Silver Malibu but couldn't see if anybody was inside.

It gave me chills to see an unusual car parked outside across from my home. I brushed it off and kept myself in my jolly mood. I guess it's a great day to be happy without a reason behind it. As the wind blew, I got through traffic with ease, listening to *Indie Aria's Conversation Album*. Her music brings me life and uplifts my spirits. I got this great feeling today, and the next upcoming days will be great. They say when happy spirits finally meet, it gives off this unexplained radiant energy.

Last night, I can honestly say I smiled and laughed with ease. A great vibe from a great person that doesn't give off, not one bad vibe all night. I just like the easy flow of how I opened up to him without thinking he would judge me. I guess it's a good thing after all. Before, leaving the neighborhood, I make my daily run to Starbucks. I decided to use the drive-thru for now instead of getting out the car today.

Realizing that I needed to change my route because if Dave can sit out and watch me, anybody could. I am one of those people who does things routinely out of habit. Turning the music up I continue with a positive approach for the day to go about my business.

Dave

Waking up feeling refreshed, I arranged to send her a gift, before going over to check on my people at my second home outside of home. I decided to have some roses delivered to Treasure's home and a basket full of scented candles. I noticed she had a few of them in her front room sitting on her entertainment center. I just hoped I don't push her away. I decided to call to check on my little brother before I got too busy. I made that an everyday commitment to talk to him or FaceTime him at least three times out the day. I know he's grown and knows how to stay safe, but all we got is each other. Calling him and the first thing out his mouth was,

"Damn bro, I didn't hear from you last night, you were in some ass laying around" he said while laughing. "You did it's about time shit; I thought you was turning a little suspect on me after you stopped dealing with ole girl," Darren respond.

"Not at all, bro ain't shit suspect about me, I just know how to keep my shit in my pants, and no, I didn't get no ass last night. I was on a first-time date with this fine ass beautiful queen," I responded.

Oh damn, does she have a sister bro" he responded as usual.

"Look at your horny ass nigga already trying to get at her sister, but no, she doesn't have any, though," I said.

"Alright, tell me about her bro she better be worth it,".

"Oh, I forgot to mention she is a paralegal," I tell him.

"Okay, bro, you always bumping into woman with careers and shit," Darren said.

"Yeah, I just have to be careful with her; she has been through something, but we just taking it slow. She agreed to go on a few more dates, so we going to see how that turns out and just go with the flow. Bro, I think I found the right one all bullshit to the side. I'll keep you posted though, how is school and work going?" I asked.

"It's all good, just a breeze, I'm just ready to be finished already so I can come home and be with my bro. I'm thinking about getting my shit together to bro because I want a family. I just got to find someone that's on my mind level and not my bank account," he gazed at me and respond.

"You will bro I know you will, but I'm about to head in here and turn my boss face on at the company. Must make sure things running smoothly, take care little bro and stay observant and stay safe; love you. I'm gone hit you up after I leave, I have some serious things to talk to you about since you are coming home soon," I said.

"Alright, bro, I be waiting for your call one love." We both say before hanging up.

I grabbed my shades and adjusted my hat and reached for my briefcase off the backseat. I get out, walk over to my door, enter the code and head straight upstairs to my office. I check the books to make sure inventory is updated and to check sales to see what's been increasing. Like always, the drinks are always on top of the list. Catering is right behind it; since business is still booming, I might just tweak the opening hours a little bit since the summer is approaching but I got to talk to my team first.

I decided to check up on my longtime friend, Dre, to see how he was doing. He was my homie, but we came from two different cloths of life. I grew up around the drug life but never was interested in it. This nigga was a true hustler, but I gave him a way out. All in high school, he used to always talk about being this best interior designer and construction worker. When I gave him his first contract he took off from there. I decided to FaceTime him since I was working.

"What's up bro, how you are doing?" I ask.

"Man, I'm blessed and highly favored, business still moving well. Just trying to find a team to help me keep it moving", Dre responded.

"That's good, keep it up, I'm sitting here checking on the business. Just had to see how you was doing, making sure you still making your name be heard," I said.

"Most definitely have to, you gave me the tools to do so," he responded.

"Keep it pushing my brother; I'm going to hit you up a little later, I said before disconnecting.

That was my A1 nigga, streets, business, and most definitely personal. Instantly, Treasure came to mind let me call her to see how her day is going. My next move is to get her an iPhone. I got to be able to FaceTime my baby at any giving time. Damn, I think I'm falling hard for her already. The chemistry we shared last night was everything. Yawl can call me a sucker I don't care. Whatever it is yawl call dudes who fall for women quick. I don't give a damn my gut isn't never been wrong, and I'm sticking with it.

"Good morning beautiful, I hope your day is going good so far, had to call you didn't get a response to my text."

"Hey there handsome, yes I did get your text this morning, I got caught up in texting my God daughter and bestie. Glad you called, how are you doing?" "I'm doing good, now that I have heard from you, I respond.

"Oh, are you, what you are doing anyhow? Oh, I'm at work checking up on things making sure things are going smooth. I'm just pulling up to work about to get the rest of my day started. Okay, sweetie, I will talk to you later, what time do you get off?" "I should be out the office by 5:30," She said.

"I was asking because I order you something that will be delivered to your door at 6:00 pm," I disclosed.

"Omg, really now you got me all anxious to get off," She responded.

"That's good. I'm going to let you go don't want you to be late, sweetie," I tell her.

"Alright, I will call you when I'm leaving out for work, Hun," she responds.

Hanging up I went back to work, making a quick run to check the supply stock and the last order placed. Everything was on point; I love my little business family they all have started with me and have stayed with me. I can't complain about life this far. I just wish my parents were here to see me and my brother become great men. Walking through the restaurant I double-checked everything before we opened. I notice a 2017 Silver Malibu parked across the street, took note of it, but didn't dwell on it too much. I head upstairs to my office and began to write down store supplies and making sure my accountant was on it. Checking to see if the last bank deposit was dropped, business is on the rise; I see thinking aloud to myself. I check the cameras to make sure they're still working and recording daily activity. As I was going over the camera's, I noticed the very same Silver Malibu the night Treasure and I came in to have dinner.

This put me on edge for a bit, and left me with a strange feeling. Checking the outside camera recording, and the vehicle wasn't there anymore. I grabbed my things to close and to get some rest from work. Pulling my shades out my pocket I put them on before setting the alarm. I'm going to have to bring it to my crew's attention to watch their surroundings and to be sure to stay on alert. I don't need any bad news happening, so I send out an email and picture of the car to Candice. I tell her to be on the lookout and make sure everyone stays safe. Getting in my car I checked my surroundings to be sure whoever it was, wasn't following me. I wasn't worried because I always kept my gun on me. Yeah, I made sure to get a conceal to carry because a man with money is always a target. I made sure to keep two inside the business as well and paid for Candice to get her own conceal to carry as well, so I wasn't worried about her not being able to handle business if the wrong situation was to occur. To my surprise, the mysteries' vehicle wasn't on site. Turning on my music to ease my mind on the drive home, I instantly thought about Treasure. Pulling up to

my home to get some rest, something was telling me to search my surroundings just to make sure the mystery vehicle wasn't following me. I sat in my car for ten minutes and decide to text her to be sure her day was going by just fine.

She responded quickly

Tre: So far; everything is going great, having lunch with my bestie.

Me: Okay, Hun just was checking on you, I'm just making it home from my business and about to shower and get some rest for work later.Be careful and know that you are a blessing to me.

She responds with the smiley love face emoji.

I get out of my car finally after not noticing anything off. Sitting my briefcase on the lazy boy I headed straight to my room to grab myself a pair of shorts. Kicking off my shoes and exchanging them for my slippers. Taking off my clothes and tossing them in my dirty clothes bin, I begin to admire my physic, not to brag, but I'm one fine ass chocolate brother. I honestly could have so many women blowing my line, but I'm not that type of person. I believe in finding love and not giving every woman that has a pussy a piece of my manhood. I don't like that people think it's okay to lie with different people and not have any attachment. Having sex brings a lot of attachment among people if people really paid that much attention to who they lay with. I believe you invite the good and bad spirits around you when it comes to laying down having sex with different people. My dad always said I reminded him of his pops with the way I carried myself. I took some time to go visit him for a week after my dad passed away and, I really do carry myself in the same manner as him. Heading in the bathroom, I turn on my iPod and let whatever play. I get in the shower and lather my body with soap, and instantly she came to mind. I can't wait to have her under me next to me at night. My manhood jumped at the thought of seeing her naked. Um, huh, let me ease my mind, forget it; I guess I can jerk off while in the shower thinking about her. Why not, so that's what I did, giving myself a damn good orgasm, leaving me feeling

relieved. Drying off after washing my body again, I decided to lay on my couch before drifting off to sleep with ease.

Treasure (Lunch-break)

Work was going by smooth; and my energy was still high. I was meeting up with Starr for lunch so I decided to walk down the street to her job to enjoy the spring breeze downtown offered. Plus, it was pointless to move my car out the lot, since I was returning to work. Walking out, I grabbed my wallet, shades, and headphones out my purse while calling Starr, letting her know I'm on my way. She let me know she would be down by the time I got there. Turning my music on, I walked down the street. The view on the way to Starr's job is so peaceful, walking across the bridge. I got there in less than ten minutes, which for me was good timing. As I reach the front of her job, her loud ass mouth was yelling out," Who got you feeling good today."

"I can't be feeling good just because I woke up feeling this way, let me find out," was my response.

"I'm just messing with you, I love the glow in you, keep it up, where are we heading to eat?", she responded.

"Something light, I got a taste for something spicy, but then I just want a salad," I respond.

"Okay, let's go to Just Salad," Starr responds. Glad that it was only a few doors down from the direction we were heading in. As we get ready to enter, I catch these sudden goosebumps, like somebody was watching me. I turn to look around before we entered and nothing out the usual. People were chatting and walking, minding their business. I brush it off once again, not letting my anxiety get the best of me. Standing in line waiting to place our order, Starr breaks the eerie feeling that comes over me.

"So, tell me about Mr. Dave; he seems like a gentleman from what you told me last night," Starr asked.

"Well, he somewhat so far is, we did a little date night to get to know each other. It turned out great; you know the restaurant I wanted to go to, well he took me there. The food is great, and the drinks they have them all. I found myself caught up in a deep

conversation with him during our date. I was able to be myself, and I opened up to him about the crazy relationship I had with Trenell.

"Wow, that's a good sign right there you were actually able to talk about it, I'm so glad you found the confidence to do so," Starr responded.

"I was amazed that I was able to discuss it with no hesitations. What are you going to eat?" I ask.

"Probably a Chicken Cesar Salad, trying to not eat so much during lunch, I promised to take Trinity out for dinner tonight," Starr responded.

"Aww, I love it, I'm ordering a spicy chicken salad," Treasure respond.

"Dave and I plan to go on more dates, just not sure if he would enjoy the same things I like," Treasured responds.

"That's the purpose of dating before committing to a relationship to get to know each other girl, stop overthinking into it. I'm pretty sure he will probably enjoy just about anything that involves being around you. I don't know if I told you but, the energy you give off is warming and welcoming to kindhearted people," Starr expressed.

Smiling from ear to ear because Starr has always kept my spirits high. I love her for being such a good friend to me. Instantly I feel someone watching me and go to look out the window and notice a gentleman standing a distance from the storefront but in the view of the window. He instantly turned around before I could get a good look at him and began walking away. I look at Starr, and she suggest that I have a seat to calm down.

"I don't need you having a panic attack on me," she says. Trying to calm myself down, I could have sworn that I just saw Trenell. Sitting down I began counting to ten, trying not to cause a scene. Starr gave me a bottle of water, and I take my time to drink it and try to relax at the same time. I just hope this man don't be on no bullshit with me if it is him. Finally, calming my nerves, I find the energy to get my food and calm Starr down enough not

to worry. I hope if that was him, he does know I have an order of protection against him by any means necessary. I have been living life breathing fresh air right until now. Let me find out he is looking for me because he finally found out about her. This is not going to be easy to get over, after all. I just knew this secret of mines wasn't gone last too long.

It's okay. I just hope I was just bugging out. Starr instantly says, "Damn, do you think he finally found out about what happened?" "Girl, my guess is as good as yours, I can't get mad if he did find out. I would have to deal with it and figure something out because I don't think he even cares about that, let's talk about my mister man though. I'm trying to stay in good spirits. I just talked to him before I went out for lunch, he says he got me a gift sent to the house later today girl," I say.

"Damn, bitch what you do to him last night for him to be buying you gifts and shit already," Starr sarcastically asked.

"Be myself, that's it, and that's all. We got a few more dates to go on before we call it official, though," I respond.

Getting to our lunch, we chow down and head out for a little walk until the last fifteen minutes of our break.

"Girl, I just hope he is for you and doesn't be like your last. I want you to be happy with someone special, and not just by yourself," Starr stated.

"My heart tells me he may be the one for me, but only time will tell, I'm not rushing it though," I respond.

"Well, let's head back on these clocks, and I'm gone call you to make sure you get there safe," Starr suggest.

Starr calls me as soon as we depart ways, back to our conversation.

"He sounds like the perfect gentlemen, I'm glad you're taking your time, I want what's best for you and if he is the one for you only time will tell," Starr countered. "Yeah, this feeling of great energy between us, I hope it stays this way. I'm surprised he got

me a gift so soon into dating, but I'm walking into the building now, hate having to cut our conversation short,

"Bitch don't thank me that's my duty to make sure you okay at all times, luckily I'm at work, or I would have had my piece on me," Starr responded.

I laughed so hard and had to let her know I would talk to her later. That girl knows she is crazy as hell, but I love her crazy ass. Heading to the elevator, calming my nerves and focusing my mind on work. I got upstairs to my office and get back to work. Ignoring what happened earlier and trying to focus on the good things in life. Deciding to take an early short vacation to clear my mind. I send in my request and to my surprise my boss approved it. So, vacation it is. Time to re-evaluate my life and take some time off and do things to keep myself focused.

Dave

My phone going off is what wakes me out of my nap. To my surprise, it's Treasure calling me. "Hey, Sweetie, what's going on?"

"Oh, nothing much just getting home from work and just

opened up the gift you got me. I love the roses, and the candles are my favorite," She says.

"Your welcome, glad to hear that you like it, I respond. How did work go today?"

"Well, I can't complain the day actually went by smooth, everything that I had to do was done on time. What are you doing for the night?" She asks.

"Well, I just woke up, about to go prep my dinner for tonight, I have to be at work by 11 pm".

"What oh my gosh, I must have hit the jackpot, giving you my number," She laughed jokingly.

"Yes, I can cook, and I enjoy it," Was my response.

"Well, I'm sorry for disturbing your rest, just wanted to let you know I received the gift," She responded.

"It's alright; I have to get up anyhow. I am glad to hear your day went by so well. Since we have agreed to go on a few more dates, I will let you pick out the next event."

"Sounds like a plan for me, but is there anything you don't like doing before I plan?" she asks.

"Not at all, I trust and hope that it doesn't have anything to do with losing my life," I responded.

She laughs and responds, "I wouldn't do anything like that to such a gentleman like you."

"Oh shit, look at the time I have to start getting ready," was my response.

"Okay, Hun, I talk to you later," She responds, disconnecting the call.

Going into the kitchen to figure out what I want to cook. I decide to do something quick and easy, not much to dig for. I take out the shrimp and chicken, deciding to make a Cajun Shrimp and Chicken Salad with a side of red beans and rice. I get to put in work in the kitchen; my favorite hobby is cooking. So, it's like music to my ears and helps me tune the outside world out if needed.

Realizing the time, it's 7:15 pm, I have to start this meal and get ready for work. Getting my night in order, I decided to record myself cooking and thought it would be nice to send it to Treasure. I recorded my every move when it comes to preparing this meal. The idea for our last date before our trip would be me inviting her over for the day and do something a little different. Yes, there are good man out here who don't think buying and spending every dollar to make a woman happy is always the way to her heart. I try my best to be different. That silver Malibu did come across my mind, not dwelling on it but, I will find out who it belongs to eventually.

Seasoning my meat, and turning the fire on, I wait for the skillet to get hot to put everything in it. While the meat is cooking, I go into the refrigerator pulling out the lettuce and season it with a little salt & pepper, chopping up my tomatoes and mixing it with the salad and cheese. I boil the water for my red beans and rice. The smell in the kitchen was making me hungry.

I notice my phone going off several times. I go check it, and it's my bro checking up on me again. I respond back to his texts and let him know; I'm alright just getting ready for work. He let me know that he will be in town for the weekend. I told him that's good news and asked if he would want to go a double date. He texted back, instantly replying to my text; he's down for it.

Bro: Okay, just show your face. He responds back; I plan to crash at your crib bro.

Me: Okay, bro, I can't wait to see you. Knowing Treasure had a friend, I ask her to see if she would like to go on a double date.

Checking on the meat tasting it, it's almost ready. Keeping the fire still going but adjusting the temperature to low. I pour my box of Zatarain's red beans and rice in the skillet. Making sure the temperature is low, I decide to hop in the shower because time was ticking. I had to make sure I had enough time to eat a little before I get to work. Taking my shower and getting ready for this night shift.

I prepare my meals. I think about the next few days being spent with Treasure. I worried myself a little bit because of her past; I don't think she will be able to deal with the other side of my personality. Trying not to ponder on it too much, I aimed not to let that side take over and control my life. After showering, I get ready for work. Leaving out for work right on time, I shoot Treasure a text to see if she wouldn't mind asking her friend if she would like to go on a double date and telling them to choose the event. Walking into the workplace, getting ready for my little night shift. The forklift isn't bad, can't complain at all, the money is good, and it's not a lot of work after all. Clocking in to make more money, easing my night.

Four

Relaxation

❧❧❧

Treasure

Waking up to Dave's text messages and his little video of him cooking. He looked like he really enjoyed cooking. He was such a gentleman but my past just wouldn't allow me to get too close to him, yet. I was feeling him though I can't lie. Reaching for my phone I call Starr and she answered on the third ring.

"Hey, there bestie, what are you doing?" I ask her.

"I'm chilling about to take this little brat to school and find something to do," Starr responded.

"I'm on my way should be there in fifteen minutes," I respond.

"Okay, I'll be waiting," she responds.

Heading out to see my God baby, after my morning run, and to chill with my bestie. Hopping in my car anxious to visit my little princess after all. I head over to go surprise her. I know she isn't expecting me to come over before she goes off to school. I get through morning traffic with a breeze.

I get to Starr's house, instead of going to the door, I tell her to send my ladybug to answer the door and don't tell her who it is. Standing smiling from ear to ear, waiting to see the look on her face when she opens the door to see me on the other side with this giant ass teddy bear in hand. I hear her running to the door. Just the sound of her little feet hitting the floor made me tear up. She

opens the door and runs out, yelling, "God-mom, is this for me. I miss you?" She asks.

"Yes, it is sweetie, and I miss you too," I respond.

Reaching to pick her up, Starr comes out, shaking her head. "You are always buying her something," she stated with a cup of coffee in hand. Walking inside and putting Trinity down so she can continue to get ready for school.

"So, what do you have planned for the weekend, and can you find a sitter for Trinity?" I ask her.

"Why are you asking a thousand and one questions, what you got up your sleeve missy," Starr states.

"I can see what I can do, but for what girl, you still haven't told me why?" She drags her voice to say.

"Oh, Dave asked me to see if you would want to go on a double date with his brother and us," I reply.

"Are you serious, stop playing with me, what is his brother like by the way," she asks.

"Well, I can tell you he is a Psychologist, and he's pursuing his Doctor's Degree to become a neurologist. So yeah, he has money, and I'm quite sure he's looking for a woman who has her own money," I respond.

Starr smart-ass had to comment and say, "Well, I hope he looks just as good as his wallet sounds."

I couldn't do anything but laugh; she is a trip. "Let's get my god baby out of here for school, before I curse you out," was my response.

Starr called Trinity to come downstairs. We head out to drop her off to school. Starr drives, I leave my car. We ended up taking a week vacation off from work after our lunch date incident. It was well needed it, especially starting off spending time with my sister and love bug. I really hope she comes out, so I decided to ask again.

"So is you gone go, we can choose the date," I ask.

31

"Girl, why would I not go? I need to get out and enjoy some male attention," Starr said. I almost broke a sweat, so use to Starr overdramatic ass saying off the wall shit out her mouth. "Do you have anything in mind," she asks?

"No, not yet, so, what is it we about to do this morning, we should go out for some relaxation. It's this place called *Spacious Spa*," I respond.

"Sounds like a very relaxing day, I'm down for it,"Starr smile's.

Arriving at Trinity's school, I get out to let her out and walk her to class, along with Starr. It's moments like this that I think about that get the best of me. I, for some reason, can't really continue to live knowing my little girl is being raised by somebody other than me. I just may go through with fighting to receive custody of my little one after all. I have to go check out what it takes to do just that during my break. Thinking to myself but slowly planning to act on it. I think this will help relieve some of my anxiety. So, after dropping off our little angel, I decided to bring the idea to Starr.

Walking out the school, "So bestie, I need your advice and opinion or something I have been thinking about lately."

Starr look at me with a side-eye and reply, "Okay sure talk to me I'm all ears and open to any advice to give honey bun."

"Well, I have been doing a lot of thinking about getting Chasity back, I know it's not going to go through as quick as I would want it to, but I'm willing to do whatever to get her in my care forever. The more I come around you and Trinity, I think about her. Should I take steps to get her back?"

Thinking to myself, I know she may have gotten comfortable with her adopted parents. "I can't live with knowing my little precious joy is in the hands of someone else. I made sure to put that in the notes; the custody agreement will be temporary due to the circumstances of how she was conceived. So, it's not like I didn't mention this before giving her up at the time." I say to Starr.

Well, I think it would be a great idea bestie just know that I'm with you every step of the way because you ell, I think it would be a great idea bestie just know and I both know it's not going to be easy," Starr responded. Making me smile just from the thought of it almost make me cry.

Breaking my thoughts, she looks at me and says, "Do you plan to tell Dave if yawl was to get serious or whatnot?"

"I didn't even think about that, and no, I haven't mentioned any of it to him yet?" I say with this dumbfounded

look…

"Okay, you said yet, so you do plan on it then, that's all that matters to me, I think it would be good to get her after all," Starr say.

Yes, she has been on my mind heavy lately, I will get around tell him," I respond.

"That's good you keep in touch with them to show that

you do care," Starr says.

"I'm glad you didn't go down my throat about it and tell me not to go along with it. I can finally stop overthinking," I tell Starr while sighing with relief.

"Have I ever gone down your throat about decisions you make, that's not my place to do so as a friend. Now let's get to this spa bath," Starr states with a bit of an attitude.

"I love you for not being judgmental. It's on eight hundred block of Superior inserting it in the GPS." I say. Starr put In the address and turn on her favorite song Good One by LA Porsha.

"So, what do you have planned for this a double date?" Starr asks.

"I was thinking something fun and out to eat afterward, probably sky-diving and out to eat if you're down for it," I respond.

"You got to be the one who wants to do the crazy shit all the time, you know what I'm down for it, it's been something on my bucket list anyhow," Starr laughs.

"It's not crazy its adventurous and memorable moments," I respond.

Come to thinking about it, I forgot I never gave him a response. So, pull my phone out of my pocket. Texting Dave, I smile.

Me: Hey there handsome I got your message I just got so

caught up into taking my Goddaughter to school and convincing Starr to join; I didn't let you know her response. She said, yeah, and we have agreed on a place to have fun and laughs and out to eat after. How do that sound? I click send.

Starr is all up in the song, and she looks over and notices I was smiling.

"Hey, see if you can get his brother number before we go out, so it won't feel too awkward between us," Starr suggests.

"That's a good idea when he responds; I will ask him," I respond. Speaking him up, he responded with a hey beautiful how is your day, and that sounds good with me, sweetie. I just hope it's fun whatever it is, he text.

I reply,

Me: Yes it will be, but Starr said do you mind if she can get your brother's name & number so they can get to know each other a little before the date, hitting send.

"Ok, so Starr, I asked him just waiting on a response," I tell her. Looking up Starr says, "Well, he going to have to wait now; we about to relax."

* * *

Realizing that we have made it to Spacious Spa. "I didn't even notice that we made it here," I say.

"Yeah, you were so busy texting and smiling," Starr said. Walking inside prepared to relax for the afternoon. I thought
this would be well worth it, after all.

"Greetings nice to meet you, how can I serve you ladies today," the front desk attendant asked.

"Give us a moment, will you," I ask.

"Alright, if you would like a tour on our service or already have the service you would like in mind, I will be here to assist you," attendant responds.

Starr, look around and suggest we take a tour of the services they have to offer.

"Alright, let's begin here is a list of services we have to offer and on the next page is where we ask that you fill out the requested info once the tour is over," the attendant says while giving us both a company tablet and stylist pen to complete the survey.

Starr ghetto ass had to be herself, "Well damn I like this place already, yawl different."

"I'm glad to hear that you do," the attendant said.

Taking the tour was a good idea because I didn't know what all they had to offer. So many different treatments, and they all sound relaxing. I like how they show you each room and on the tablet display what happens and still take the time to give a tour. They don't let the use of having electronics take over everything, which is good. I didn't want to take up all of Starr's time today while Trinity was in school, so something simple will do.

"Star, what service do you plan on getting," I ask her.

"Oh, girl, I'm trying to relax and do a little shopping today for Trinity and me," she says.

"Okay, so let's do the full body massage with drinks & a relaxing bath," she agrees.

The tour was over with after five-ten minutes, "So have you ladies decided on what service you would like, and if so, do you prefer the same room or separate," asked the attendant.

"Oh, same room will be perfect.. right, Starr," I said, allowing her to give her opinion.

"Now you know I want to be able to chit chat with my bestie and relax at the same time," Starr says.

"Alright, ladies, let me step out for a second to let the masseuse know and prepare the room for the both of you. While I'm helping prepare would you guys kindly fill out the survey using the link at the bottom of the tour guide," the front desk attendant asked.

Starr look up from watching the video for the full body massage and bath, before smiling. As the attendant left the room, Starr silly ass laughs this dramatic annoying laugh that she usually does when she has something mischievous, better yet kinky thoughts. "You up for some fun after this," she asks.

"Starr, what kind of fun do you have in mind because that laugh is only when you up to something out the ordinary and it's no telling with you," I ask.

"Well, I was thinking let's hit up *Pleasure Play* store," Starr suggests.

"Okay, sure, with your kinky ass, you trying to get you some soon, damn get to know the man first." I laugh out loud and try to whisper to Starr at the same time.

"Who says I get somethings for him, how you just gone figure I'm throwing the cat at him like that. Seriously, I'm going for myself and getting a few other items; I'm trying to spice up my next relationship cause I'm making it my last and ready to settle missy," Starr responds.

Standing in shock with my mouth wide open, I was surprised to hear my bestie say she trying to make this her last relationship and turn it into something meaningful. Touching her forehead with the back of my hand to check to see if she had a fever, my sarcastic ass.

"Are you feeling okay today, did you fall or hit your head on the nightstand," I ask.

"Bitch, now you overdoing it," eyes rolling and giving her the stare of death.

"Excuse me," disrupting the unpleasant conversation among us the front desk attendant return and giving us both a key to place our belongings in a locker; she guides us to the shower room. Noticing the awkward silence, she asks, would we like a glass of wine now or while in the bath.

To my surprise, in unison, we both respond, "Now, please!"

Looking over at Starr, hesitate to say anything else to her. I wait until she makes eye contact, and she does just as I thought. She walks over to me and whispers in the most spiteful tone. "Don't insult me like that again in public or we gone box it out on our next girls date out for real bitch," and burst out laughing.

"You just sounded like a psychopath," I laugh along.

"That's good because I was serious," she responds.

"Anyhow losing up, I was only joking you still don't know when I'm being sarcastic," I say.

Departing to go get changed into our bathrobes, thoughts of my little bundle of joy begin to run through my mind. I miss her truly; I just hate that I didn't give it shot to raise her from birth like I should have. Checking my phone to see if Dave ever responded back. Sure, enough he did and with no questions asked, he sent his brother info, and I happily copied and sent it to Starr. Following behind that texts was a text he sent, I hope your bestie/sister can deal with my brother after all. He is quite the charmer I can say. Hey, maybe they will click after all thinking to myself. Placing my belongings in my locker and returning to get my wine that was waiting.

Starr come out the room with this Kool-Aid smile across her face, "Girl, it's time to bring out my classy side of me and throw the ratchet bitch away. Mister man is fine as fuck, and he is very intriguing. So far, he likes what he sees I sent him my natural me as in now look and my beauty as far as work or going out look. He loved my natural look a lot better. He got a chick thinking; I should just stick with my natural after all, just eyeliner and my lashes," Starr states while twirling her hair.

That was quick I hope you guys actually progress," I tell her. We head to the room to begin are a moment of relaxation. My mind instantly drifts into ease, but thinking about my baby girl, and this long process it's going to take to get her back in my arms. Relaxing my mind and thinking happy thoughts. Looking over at Starr, she looks relaxed. Enjoying the rest of the relaxing moment after thirty minutes, it was time for full-body massages. To my surprise, it was two handsome gentlemen waiting for us. "Hey, Tre, you looked like you was pretty relaxed; how was it for you babes," Starr asked.

"I enjoyed it, my little angel been on my mind heavily, but overall it was relaxing.

"How was it for you? How do you feel?" I ask.

"Baby, this wine and that lite soak bath was relaxing as hell, honey," she responds.

Leaving the bath getting ready to receive the best part of the treatment. Getting ready to get the kinks and knots out removed. The masseuse gives us a tray of chocolate-covered infused strawberries and ask that we lay stomach flat on the tables. Using two different oils that we choose during the beginning of the tours. I decided to use the lavender oil that's for relaxing and relieving tension. The smell in the air was lavender aromatherapy mixed with the orange spice mixed with a cinnamon aroma. It created a pleasant smell in the room with such a soothing vibe.

The masseuse begins to glide his hands across my neck, knocking out every bit of tension. He takes his time to work his way down to my luscious thick thighs. He knew exactly what he was doing, and thanks to him, I left the spa feeling great and relaxed. Before leaving we paid for the service after the session, and I tip the masseuse for doing such a great job. Neither of them was expecting such a generous tip giving by us. The front desk attendant gave us a discount card to use for couples treat. Trying

to keep up with Star and trying to reply back to Dave's texts. He had texted me several times during my spa treatment.

Star turns around, realizing I got my face glued in my phone. "Can you put your phone up for a chance at least until we're done with our date," Starr whines.

"You're lucky I love you because if I didn't, this phone would still be glued to my fingertips and my face all in it," I sarcastically reply. Sending my last message to Dave, letting him know I will text him later.

* * *

Walking into Pleasure Play, Starr grabs my hand to follow behind her. The first thing she picked up is two pairs of fur handcuffs, and some edible lick me off gels. Pick two flavors you may like; I don't want to hear nothing else," Starr said. Checking out the flavors they have, I pick up the Strawberry and Peach flavors edible gels. Starr snatches them from me and tosses them in her basket. I go over to the area for

vibrators and pick me up two different kinds.

"Uh-huh, you little nasty," causing me to jump Starr says out of nowhere.

"I used to keep me a couple of these things all the time got to keep her from purring," I respond with a smirk.

Starr looks at me and smile, "I knew it was in you, see you one of them behind closed door freaks, that's why crazy wasn't trying to let you go."

"Oh, my goodness, gasping at Starr's statement. Okay, after all these years, yes girl, your sister is a freak, freak," I reply while laughing at her. Shaking my head, I knew it had to be a reason why that man was so damn infectious with you," Starr snickers.

"If I knew he was crazy, I never would have given up the cookie to his ass in the first place." Treasure reply.

"I'm glad that you can actually joke about it without feeling depressed," Starr states. Looking at her and smiling.

"It's because you have helped me to do just that, I tell her.

"That's why we are besties, now let's finish shopping," Starr states while reaching for a dildo.

"Don't you have enough of them things already, you should have a dresser full by now," I said.

"No, I buy new ones and get rid of the old ones, I don't keep a collection of them unless they all have different purposes," Starr stated while sucking her teeth.

"Let's get out of here and go find some outfits for this weekend and get my baby cakes some clothes," I suggested.

Heading to the front of the store, Starr picks up some blindfolds and lubricants. The cashier looked at us and smiled while ringing up our products. I look up, and Starr winked her eye at her. The young lady probably thought we were just some full-blown freaks.

Walking out the store, Starr burst out laughing. Looking at her with this crazy expression on my face not knowing what she was laughing at, she whispers in my ear. As we walk out the storefront and say, "I winked my eye at the cashier, and I guess it gave her the impression we were a couple," Starr says.

"That's why she was smiling at me like that, Starr your ass plays entirely too much for me," I say.

She grabs my hand and licks my neck, and it leaves a warm tingling feeling behind. Reaching for my neck and looking at Starr. "Wait, what did you put on my neck?" Reaching for a wipe and some sanitizer from my purse waiting for Starr to respond.

Oh, nothing it got you uh feeling some type of way," Starr laughs. See this was the silly college girl Starr that use to work my nerves, but I love it she's keeps me laughing and enjoying life no matter if it's out eating or shopping. "Just know I got you

some that you can use for mister man." Starr reaches in her bag and drops the bottle in my bag.

* * *

Making our way to *Children's Place* to get ladybug Trinity some clothes. The first thing I spotted was a few cute little spring dresses for her. Starr finds her some outfits for school and some shoes. Leaving *Children's Place* and to find these weekend outfits for us.

Deciding I would wear something comfortable a fitted sweat suit would be perfect. I grabbed some high waist ripped jeans, and some plain ones just to have. Starr grabs a sweat suit as well. I take my purchases to the register and check out.

I leave and go into Victoria Secrets every woman's addiction. I ended up spending almost two hundred dollars on two bras and four pairs of panties alone. Starr comes smiling and singing her way inside Victoria Secret as I was getting ready to walk out. "I knew I would find your ass in this damn store; let me grab a few underwear and we can call this therapy date over with," Starr says.

"Okay, I will be waiting over here," pointing to the closets sitting area.

Plopping my big ass down in the chair and watching a couple with this beautiful little girl take random pictures caught my attention. The little girl looked a lot like my crazy ex. Coming to my senses; I realized the little girl was my precious angel Chasity. Tears begin to fall down my face, I get up to walk toward the family, and something stops me. I couldn't find the courage to push my feet forward. Tears flow down my cheeks at a rapid pace; they look so happy together.

* * *

The woman looks over at me and smiles and then double looked again as she reached to grab her hand. I look down to see that she had a baby bump, and she walked towards me. I reach for some Kleenex to wipe my eyes, and she extends her arms out to me and gives me a huge hug with open arms. It's shocking to me because even though I see my ex in my beautiful little girl, she resembles me so much. I ask the couple if I could take a picture of her, and sure enough, they allowed me to. We exchanged numbers, and she

asked me if my address or email was the same because she had sent several emails with no response. I let her know I haven't checked my personal email in a while. She let me know they will be throwing her first birthday party and would like for me to attend. I let them know I will gladly be there. The wife tells me to check my email and get in touch with them as soon as possible before departing. I promise her soon as I get home, I will.

I can't believe I was able to get in touch with them at such a time. I cry tears of joy after watching them leave the mall.

Starr walks out of Victoria Secret, and the first thing she say is,

"What's wrong with you."

"You won't believe it God works in mysterious ways I can tell you that." Wiping tears from my eyes, unlocking my phone, handing it to Starr.

"Oh, my God she starts crying, she is beautiful where she at, did you just see her?" She asks.

"Yes, I did," I respond.

"Stop lying, are you serious what did you say and what did she do?" She asked.

"I'm so serious Starr, I'm still in shock, and I didn't say much to her, I took the picture and spoke the wife. She asked me to check my email and invites me to come to her first birthday party, we exchanged numbers, and I let her know I would check my email and will be there for her first birthday."

"It's weird because right before you got here, we were just having the discussion about you wanting to get her back in your care," Starr responded.

"Yes, it does, and I'm a firm believer everything happens for a reason," I respond. Now feeling overwhelmed with joy after seeing my precious little angel, I was anxious to get back home. I didn't want to be rude, so I continue my date with my bestie. Leaving Victoria secrets, making our way to the food court.

So how do you feel after actually seeing her again?" Starr ask.

"I am not gone, lie sis. I feel excited and overwhelm. I think it was really meant for this to happen. I can't wait to get home to see what it is she has sent me," I respond.

"Well, let's get back to my place so you can get home," Starr suggests. Leaving the food court, we head out to the car. Before going our separate ways, we head to go get Trinity from school. Feeling relaxed and overjoyed hanging out today was refreshing and a happy moment. The drive to Starr's house was peaceful, I guess Trinity was tired because soon as she got in the car, she was knocked out. Starr checked the time and starts grinning from ear to ear. I guess the connection between her and Darren so far is good. As we get in front of her home, we hug, exchange gifts, and I kiss my Goddaughter.

Getting in my car, the tears just run down my face nonstop. I just can't believe life truly has its purpose for playing out the way you want it when you least expect it to. Calming my nerves counting to ten before pulling off. I open my sunroof and allow the spring breeze to help me stay calm. Taking I-57 home, I get home in no time, but being hesitant even to check my email, I decided to take a shower. After my shower, I light a few candles and head over to my mini office.

* * *

Checking my email as I promised, taking my time to do so. To my surprise, it's more pictures of my little angel Chasity and, at the very end, is a letter to reconsider her adoption due to the family having twins on the way unexpectedly. I couldn't do anything besides cry tears of joy and excitement. The family was told a few years ago they wouldn't be able to have children of there own, which is the many reasons they considered adoption. Being the circumstances of how Chasity was conceived, I was able to give her up for temporary or permanent adoption. I was so thankful for the couple and forever grateful that they even considering to allow me to raise my baby girl myself. Taking the rest of the evening to
go over the paperwork, signing and sending it back to them as requested.

Deciding to take the time out tomorrow to give them a call and to schedule a time to go over things. I decide to meditate and chill for the night with a movie until I knock out for the night. The gift of glory things happens in a timely matter.

Dave

I found myself spending most of my day running errands to get some basic supplies for the restaurant and keeping in touch with Treasure today. Using some time just to relax and chill, I realized I just hooked my brother up on a semi-blind date out the blue. I just hoped they would click; with that being said, I decided to text him.

Me: Hey, bro, so how do you like her so far?

I click send, and wait for his response. I decided to find my wardrobe for the weekend events.

To my surprise, he calls, "Hey bro, she so far seems cool she's beautiful and knows how to keep a conversation going," He states.

"That's good bro I just thought about it and had to see what's to it, I knew she didn't have any sisters, but she told me she had a best friend," I tell him.

"So, you ready for this weekend bro, I kind of like how you make your second date a double date. With your slick ass, always doing some shit. Maybe we can take a trip out of state as a celebration if we make it official as another double date. If me and this beautiful queen make it to that level," Darren said.

"True, without a doubt, bro, it will be well worth it, after all," I say.

"The only thing is that she has a little girl, so I have to be very sure of my decision once making it, bro," Darren said with concern.

"Take it easy, and in due time she will introduce you to her daughter if she feels it's right, bro, so don't panic," I tell him.

"You right about that, I will be out there tomorrow bro so be easy. Love you," Darren responds.

"Okay, I'm about to go downstairs and workout for an hour before I rest for work tonight, love you too and talk to you later," I respond.

Disconnecting our call I headed downstairs to my man cave. Trying to keep the focus on my workout, I continue for thirty more minutes before ending it to take a nap.

Five

Time With Love Ones

Dave

I was chilling waiting on my brother to make it out here. I decided we should go out and hang out like old times just the two us. Reaching out to Treasure to see how her day was going was my usual way of starting my morning since meeting her. It's something about communicating with her before starting my day, that keeps me going. I sent her a GIF and a morning text, so she knew I was thinking of her. The texts read,

Me: "Good morning, beautiful sending you blessings and happy energy to start your morning with ease. Thinking of you early today can't wait to enjoy spending time with you this weekend. Call me when you not so busy, yours truly."

* * *

I decided to take the time to cook myself breakfast this morning instead of ordering out and was debating on what to cook. I go into the kitchen, searching the refrigerator and pull out the bacon, eggs, and bread to make French Toast, with some strawberries on the side. Turning on my music grooving to the sounds of some hood music.

"Okay, bro, I see you; she got you in the kitchen cooking and shit," Darren walked in the kitchen and said.

"Oh, shit, man, I keep forgetting you have keys to my crib. I almost pulled out the burner, what up bro you here earlier than expected,"

I respond after realizing it was him at the door.

"True, I see I'm right on time for breakfast, though," Darren respond, while going to the refrigerator to grab something to drink.

"Bro I had to get here early didn't want to be caught in traffic, plus I wanted to kick my big brother tonight," Darren respond, while popping a can of beer open.

"I'm let that slide, you gone be the same way soon," I tap his shoulder, walking out the kitchen with my plate. "Hold on, where my plate at?" Darren ask.

"You on your own playboy fix it yourself; everything is done," I respond. Reaching for my phone I noticed Treasure texted back.

Treasure: Good morning, I have a productive morning ahead of me still on vacation from work but got business to handle glad to hear from you.

Me: Okay that's good, finish your day I will get in touch later. Attaching the picture of my breakfast with the caption I will fix breakfast for you like this soon, on a daily. Breakfast in bed style.

"Aww, man, don't tell me you posting your food on Facebook, bro," Darren laughed.

"Not this meal, bro, but you know that's how a business stays going up. I sent this to Treasure telling her if she was here, she could have breakfast daily," I respond with a smile. "You fucking cornball ass nigga," Darren said while laughing trying not to choke.

"It's my way of letting her know, I'm always thinking of her. Hell, it's called keeping her interested," I tell him.

"What you got planned for us tonight we should hit up the gentleman's club they just opened up and go shoot some pool for the night out," Darren said, smiling.

"Cool sounds like a plan," I respond.

Enjoying the last of my breakfast and deciding to go to the gym to get an early workout. I leave my brother in the house, no need for him to tag alone; he probably was tired anyhow.

Treasure

I remember that I didn't let Starr know I made it home safe. Up and out taking care of business this morning.

I call Starr, "Morning dear my fault for not letting you know I made it home safe. I came in, took a shower and opened my email, and was just overjoyed with the news I had received," I instantly respond. "It's okay Hun, so what was the good news," She asks.

Well, when I first opened the email it was several pictures of Chasity, and at the end was a letter. The wife how much they adored Chasity, but felt it would be best for her to return home. Due to the fact that the having twins they felt it would cause Chasity to have a lot of unanswered questions. Besides, it was a temporary custody and they felt it was time for her to return to me," I explain to Starr.

All I hear on the end of the phone, is Starr sniffling sounding as if she was crying, "Oh my god, it's really meant for you to have her back in your care," Starr says while blowing her nose. I know it is stop crying, you gone make me cry, I'm dropping off picking Trinity up from school, so go find you something to do," I tell Starr.

"Okay, that's fine with me can you drop her off to her grandparents in the morning for the weekend?" "Sure, I got you love enjoy. I will see you tomorrow," I hang up and continue my day. Deciding to spend some time with my God-daughter today would ease my mind a little.

Calling Dave to ease my mind, right now would a good idea. Not realizing he texted me again, I check it and smile. It's a pic of his breakfast he cooked and a text stating how I could be feed breakfast like this daily.

He answers the phone quick, "Hey, beautiful, what's up how you doing?"

"Hey, there just finish running some errands and noticed your text from earlier needed to hear your voice," I respond.

46

"Oh, really, that sounds like in other words, you miss me," smiling over the phone he responds.

"If you say so, I guess," I respond.

"What are you doing?"

"At the gym, working on was about to go take a swim before you called. I can't wait to see you tomorrow though feels like forever since we last saw each other," he responds.

"It hasn't been that long at all just a few weeks, but I just hope yawl don't chicken out on us though," I say.

"Why would I do that?" He asked.

"Well, just say the date will be pretty fun a little adventurous," I tell him.

"That's what's make it even better; I like surprises we will be there for sure though." He says.

"This is more excited than I thought after all; wear something comfortable no fancy stuff. I'm let you get back to your workout." I respond.

"Okay Hun thanks for the heads up, I will talk to you later." He responds and ends the call.

Dave

Thinking to myself, What the hell did I get me and bro into with this double date. Oh, well, I can't change my mind now. Before taking my swim, I texted Darren and let him know I should be home in a few. Using my last hour in the gym to take a swim and calling it enough for the day. Taking a quick shower before leaving the gym, ready to get home to eat lunch and rest for a bit. I took my time gathering myself before leaving the gym. I guess going out with my brother tonight will be worth it. Getting in my car I cruised through traffic with ease. Making it home in no time, I opened the front door, and to my surprise, my bro was asleep. Growling, the loud sound my stomach made let me know that I was hungry. Heading to the kitchen to find something to eat, I decided to fix something light. I prepared myself homemade bacon cheeseburgers and fries. Getting sleepy after my little meal and take a nap so I can be ready for tonight's events.

Treasure

Deciding to go home and meditate for a little until it's time to pick up Trinity. Chasity starts to come to mind instantly.

Thinking to myself, how will I tell Dave about her. Only in due time, I will have to eventually. Depending on how things will go between us anyhow. Finally making it home, not rushing to get out my car, I notice a Silver Malibu slowly pulling in behind me. Not trying to overreact or assume whoever it is could be following me. I get out of my car in a rush to get inside. The driver pulls off before I could turn around to get a good look to see who it was. Hastily, but not trying to panic, I rush to get inside and quickly set my alarm. Pacing the floor before going any further into my house, I began counting aloud to calm my nerves. Thinking to myself, maybe it was just someone with the wrong address. Trying to clear

my overthinking mind, after all, I have been quite nervous lately about things.

Lighting my candles in my front room while heading to fix me some tea. I grab my remote to my sound-bar and play my music to ease my racing mind. Heading into the kitchen to fill my tea kettle with cold water and placing it on the stove. I go to take out my favorite teacup and place my lemons and yoga passionate flavor tea bag inside. Pulling out my fruits from the refrigerator, I take my time to create a nice small fruit salad and placing some up for Trinity to have later. Twirling through my home while eating the fruit was an unexpected relief for me. My mind was clear again; without a doubt, I have found a lot of ways to ease my mind after going through an abusive relationship for three years. It can put you through a lot, mentally. The loud whistling noise of my tea kettle startles me out of my little meditation. Making my way to the kitchen to turn the kettle off, I do just that. Pouring the water into my already prepared cup, the smell of the tea releases. Deciding I will take a nap until it's time to pick up Trinity. I instantly drift off to sleep on the couch.

Evening

Awaking from my nap. It's close to the time for me to pick up Trinity from school. Grabbing my car keys, and heading out to her school. Getting there on time, I park my car across the street. Make my way to her classroom. I walk in the classroom and she notices me before I could even finish signing her out. She runs to me, and I pick her up and embrace. "So, how was school today sweetie?" I ask her. She looks at me, "School was good, where is my mama?" She ask.

"She's at home would you like to call her?" I ask.

"Yes, she says while smiling. I call Starr through FaceTime.

"Hey, chick what's going one," she answers.

"Trinity was wondering where are you that's all, I think you should have let her know I was picking her up," I respond while giving Trinity the phone.

She talks to her mom briefly and gives me the phone after disconnecting the call.

"Do you want to go to movies and see Frozen 2?" I ask while putting her in her favorite car seat.

"Yes, that would be so fun, can we go now," she ask.

"Sure," I reply.

We go to AMC theaters, and I buy get us popcorn and slushes, before we go find are seats.

"When we leave we're going to go to McDonald's to eat and go to my house and play in paint beautiful pictures," I tell her.

"Yah, she jumps up and down with excitement in her eyes, mom don't let me paint at home because we have carpet everywhere," she says.

"Well you can at my house anytime you like," I assure her.

We get to the theater where the movie has just started. Enjoying the movie, Trinity the entire time has the biggest smile on her face. The ending of the movie was interested, we throw are trash away and go straight to McDonald's. I order Trinity, a happy meal, and myself a Chicken tender meal to go. I let her eat in the car, something I had a habit of doing. We arrive to my house and I noticed the same Silver car I thought I saw before. I rush inside with Trinity in my arms and lock the door. We enjoyed the rest of are night, ending it with giving her a bathe and like always she fall asleep with ease.

Dave

Time to go out and enjoy the night with my brother. Preparing my outfit for the night, I decided to cook a little dinner to save us a few bucks. So after grabbing my things out to wear, I head to the kitchen to take something out to cook. "Aye, bro, you want to eat something before we go ahead," I yell out to him. "Sure, why not, it's worth it save me money," Darren responds. With that being said, I take the Cube Steaks, and for the sides some Asparagus and Spanish rice. Darren walks in the kitchen and heads to the fridge to grab another beer. I look at him and shake my head, thinking to myself, He gone be lit before we can even make it out to enjoy ourselves. Let me get this dinner prepared so we can get ready. Preparing dinner, I turn on the music and get to work my magic. We eat dinner and get ready to go out.

Night out bro

Deciding to go shoot pool first and talk shit and grab a drink. We head over to the bar. I order two pitchers of beer and a bottle of Hennessy. We head downstairs to the pool table.

Taking my first cup for the night, I chug one down and said, "Hell, Bro, I'm trying to feel how you are feeling you been drinking since you got in."

"Now you know I have a high tolerance for alcohol, plus its beer. I piss that shit right out," Darren responds.

"Let's get this game of started you go first," I respond.

"I don't know why you let me go first, you know I'm a pro at this, I'm not coming off this table," Darren responds while setting the rack up. He talks so much shit it's ridiculous, but he wouldn't be him if he didn't. "White ball," he yells instantly shoots two in.

"I guess you got lucky this time around keep going you gone miss," I respond.

"We will see about that bro let's play best out of three if I win you have to pay my car note next month," Darren said.

"Okay deal if I win you have to make Starr your only girl and really get to know her and run my restaurant for a month," I tell him.

"Bet, deal that's cool with me," Darren responds while pouring a shot in his glass.

"You gone lose fool. I can't wait, plus to see you go thru with this bet gone be the best part about it," I respond.

"Quit talking shit nigga before I make sure you lose on purpose because I can use a break off paying my car note for a month," Darren responds. "I know the biggest shit talker isn't trying to tell me to quit talking shit, let me find out bro scared of falling in love," I respond. Times like this spent with my brother are what I love the most like we are the total opposite, but we know how to keep each other going.

"I'm not scared of falling in love; I just don't want to start nothing that won't last long that's all. Like bro, I just want to

build a connection with someone that is different from what I've been dealing with, that's all," Darren respond.

"I feel you bro that is understanding to especially for a man in your predicament," I say to him.

"Damn, bro, you distracting me," Darren said aloud.

He ends up missing the next shot.

"Don't blame me, bro, and you better not quite either," I respond. Taking my time knocking in four balls, one after another and laugh.

"It's cool we got two more games to play don't get geek," Darren said.

"I have to with you bro because you talk a lot of shit, and you know me, I always got to prove you wrong every time," I say. Chalking up my cue to take another shot and two cue balls goes in and leave me with a direct hit for the next shot to go in hopefully without scratching. Hurry up and miss bro so I can get this hot five hundred out of you," Darren responds.

"We gone see about that playboy, come next round because this one you not winning," I say. Chalking my cue stick to go

again and trying not scratch, and damn, that's all I needed.

"Yeah, get your ass out the way it's my turn to take over," Darren was quick to say.

"Man, we got two rounds to go quit talking tough tony," I respond. He chalks up his cue stick and aims to the closets target; three balls go in back to back. Thinking to myself, he just might win after all. I am not gone; let him, though, give him a run for his money. He ended up making all balls in he have the eight ball left to win.

"Yeah, bro, you got my money right; I don't want to hear no excuses after these next two ass win," Darren say.

"I'm a man of my word, bro, so you gone get it if you win," I respond.

* * *

We knock the next two games out with a breeze, and true enough, he wins. I instantly give him his money to not hear his mouth. Leaving and getting ready to go to *Ocean's Gentleman Club.* Pulling into the parking lot and I instantly notice the Silver Malibu that was outside of my restaurant. I ignore it due to me not knowing who it belongs to. Entering the club, we get VIP treatment, due to me knowing the owner. He sends over his best dancers to me and my brother, that goes by the name of Daisy and Desire twin sister's. The bartender brings over a special bottle of Hennessy, and on the side of the bottle was a tag that reads, On the house, don't worry about. Darren requested a hookah and pours himself a drink. He reaches into his pocket before sitting down enjoying the mood. The girls instantly put on a show and me and bro gladly drop a few blue faces and singles for their service. Not feeling the VIP area I went out to the floor, and it's going down. All you see is ass hanging from poles and breasts out. I get caught into a chick who was sparking up flames using a candle in her pussy. It was mesmerizing to see what breaks my attention is some idiot pushed me. I had to keep myself from falling because he damn near knocked me over.

"Bro watch where you're going before, we have a problem," I yell.

He looks at me with this look of confusion and say, "We already have a problem, and you don't even know it," and he walks off.

I had to see where he was heading with this. Following behind him trying to keep up, I end up losing him in the crowd. I go outside to see if I can locate him and no sight of him. I realize the Malibu is not in view at all. Thinking to myself, I need to get to the bottom of this for real, for real. This shit has gotten to me seriously. Heading back inside the club and before making my way back to my brother, a drop shorty how had my attention before my little altercation a few bills. Making my way back to my brother, I grab the bottle and take a huge drink out of it. Relaxing my mind and chilling for the rest of the night, I get back

to enjoying my night. Not wanting to get my brother all rallied up, I didn't even mention the issue with him. Just continued with are night out of enjoying the company of my brother.

Six

Double Date

~✥~

Treasure

After, enjoying a night of fun with my goddaughter, it was
Friday and time to get ready for me and my bestie to go with the guys
tonight. I had already dropped Trinity off with her grandparents, as requested
by Starr. I decided to go over her house, and we would just get ready and
leave out together and meet up with Dave and Darren. Thinking to myself,
I can't believe I set my friend up to go on a blind date, and she is actually
looking forward to it. I guess some people actually do better with blind dates
better than others after all. Making it to Starr's house in no time, and I text
her to open the door.

Getting out my car and going to my truck to crib my carry-on bag with my
clothes in it. Starr comes outside with this Kool-Aid grin plastered across her
face. Thinking to myself, I hope and pray he is the one for her and that he is
perfect for my goddaughter. I just want her to be happy in life with someone
who is right for her. Walking into her home, I ask her, "So you ready for this
adventurous day of fun and excitement," I ask her.

"Now you know I'm more than ready I just got off the phone with him he says they're getting ready," Starr respond.

"Okay, well, we need to get ready," I say. Starr was already heading to the bathroom before I could even ask her anything else. Taking the time to text Dave letting him know I can't wait to see him. I prepare my clothes to get ready.

Waiting on Starr, to come out of the bathroom, I turned on some music. "That's my jam girl turn it up," She yells. I do just that. She comes out of the bathroom ten minutes later, shaking her ass. I make my way to the bathroom with my belongings to take a shower. Placing my things on the stand in the bathroom, I turn on the removing shower head and take my shower. Getting ready to get out, Starr burst open the door, asking me how did she look.

"Damn, you could've waited to tell I came out look good and just right for the event," I respond. She puts her hair in a messy bun and walks out of the bathroom. I look at my hair and shake my head, not realizing what I want to do with my hair since I had my hair cut in a pixie cut. A look I have been wearing since I left Trenell crazy ass. I had to find myself and change somethings, and so I started with my hair. I love my short hair, but I think I'm going to grow it back after all. Covering my body with my Shea buttercream I prepared myself to dress. I come out and grab my makeup bag.

Heading into Starr's room to see what she was doing, and to my surprise, her ass was in the mirror taking selfies. I noticed she had already put her makeup on, which was more of the natural look instead of the work look she usually wears. She final turn to look my way "Bitch that sweat suit is fitting and looks damn good on you," she smiles while posting on snap chat. "Thanks, bestie, I'm almost ready we can leave out if your ready," I say to Starr.

"Yeah, I'm ready when your ready," Starr reply.

With that being said, we grab our wallets and phone deciding not to carry purses. On this adventurous date a purse wasn't needed. Debating for a few minutes on who will drive, we decided that I will.

Getting into my car putting the location into the global positioning system tracker, that I had put in my car after receiving it. It kept me from using my phone. Off to begin are adventurous double date. Thinking to myself, I don't know if I'm more excited to go or to see the connection between my bestie and Darren or the date in general. Starr turns on the Bluetooth connection and blasts

Cardi B, She Bad. Her ratchet side was out, and she was ready to enjoy herself. Taking the drive to Chicagoland Skydiving Center. Giving stay the address to send to Darren, and the first thing she is burst out laughing. "Girl Darren texted me saying what the hell kind of date is this, saying we trying to kill him," Starr says.

Laughing, "Tell him what he scared it's fun and something out of the normal," I say. She texted him.

"Dave says to tell you your very adventurous, and they heading there now," Starr say.

"Tell them we will see them there; we on our way as well, and we are going to have fun," I tell her.

Making it there in good timing before they could actually get there, which was a good thing. Deciding to text Dave to see how long will it take them to arrive, before I could hit send on the texts, I notice his car in the distance coming our way. Waiting for them to park, I turned to

Starr smiling and had to ask her, "How do you feel, girl?"

"I'm good, you know me, let me stop lying, girl, I'm nervous as shit," Starr said.

"I know your facial expression shows it; you're in good hands," I reassure her.

Looking up to check my lips and putting on more lip gloss. Dave startles me, walking up on me from behind and wraps his strong arms around my waist and turns my face to face to him. Looking up at him causes me to smile like a kid in a candy store, he reached for my face and gave me a passionate hug and kiss. Whispering in between kisses that he missed me. I don't know, but what's weird I don't catch the butterflies or have that jittery feeling like a little school girl. His presence does have me feeling relaxed and safe when he's around. Turning around to introduce Dave to Starr, I had to interrupt them.

"Well, Starr not to be rude, but this is Dave, and Dave this Starr, my best friend," I say.

Dave speaks and introduces his brother to me, and we didn't bother to introduce Darren and Starr to each other because they had already done that.

"Alright, is you'll ready to go on this adventure of skydiving?" I ask.

"Let's go put our lives and some strangers hand," Darren sarcasm kicks in.

Starr snickers like a schoolgirl, and sticks her tongue out at me.

Dave grabs my hand, and we head inside to prepare for the adventure awaiting us.

Darren and Starr follow behind us, from the looks of it seem like they will get along just fine.

Making our way inside the instructor greets us and asks, are we ready to get suited and booted. Showing us an instruction video and going over the steps on how to release the parachute for proper precautions. Taking the time to make sure we were clear on what to do.

We all get paired with our own assistant that will guide us thru and help us make the drive safely. Starr had to be the one to crack the jokes, and to my surprise, Darren finished them off. Giggling so hard, my stomach starts to hurt. Having us all laughing so hard we had to get back focused while on the helicopter heading to the jumping area. The fun part about the jump we all were taking the time to go one after the other and not together. I choose to go first since it was my idea to come here. The assistant says, "At one we're jumping so brace yourself and keep your finger on the parachute button, we're all going to release the parachutes at the same time after everybody has jumped out," the assistant explains. "Alright, counting down five, four, three, two, one and ready."

Before you know it, we're in the sky; the adrenaline rush was satisfying. It turned out to be a great experience after all, and bucket list event well worth it. Once we landed, we met up, and to my surprise, everybody's reactions were the same as mine.

"That was fun more excited than I thought, how about we go one rounder, and we take pics," Dave assists.

"Sure, it's worth it; why not I guess it is okay to do things out of the normal to experience what life has to offer after all," Darren responds. "Let's go another round I down for it," Starr said.

Guiding us back to the area, we prepare for another dive out of the helicopter. This time with excitement, we get ready for a second dive of fun. We were actually able to take pics and make silly faces without being so nervous. The assistant took the pics as we embraced the moment of it all. Making it to the target, the assistant snaps more pics as we land, and once we all got it together, he let us know that they will go and print out the pics and have them ready in just a few minutes.

Going back to the main building to return the gear and receive the pictures, Dave pulls out his card and makes the payment instantly on his tab. Reaching for my waist, "I hope you didn't think I was gone let you pay when I the one that asked you?" he whispers in my ear.

"I really didn't think about that," I say while putting my card back inside my wallet.

"That was a good now we do yawl crazy adventurous woman got us going to next, I'm not down for anymore jumping out planes and shit right now," Darren respond.

"Well, I'm glad you were willing to continue even though it wasn't something you were really up to doing, but did you enjoy yourself?" Starr ask.

"Sure, I did enjoy myself after all," Darren says.

"Well, the next is just out to shoot some pool, drink and eat, just the usual fun," Treasured states.

"Oh, okay, this will be fun after all, I just beat Dave ass in a game of pool last night, Ha, ha, ha laughed Darren.

"Alright, now no need to brag," Dave responds.

"Let's go get the rest of this day going," Starr interrupts.

"Okay, well how about I drive your car bro, and you and Starr switch," Darren suggests.

"Sounds like a plan," agreeing with Darren, Treasure tossed her keys to Dave.

"Aye, bro, we gone follow behind," Darren says.

Heading to the cars after receiving the pictures and discounts to come again, we depart. Getting into my car with Dave driving, I give him the location of where we're going, and we drive off.

"Wow, what an experience that was I really enjoyed it a lot. You are one adventurous woman I see," Dave said.

"I just like to enjoy the things a lot of people don't like to do; it makes the best experience in life," Treasure respond. "True, so what are your thoughts so far about me," Dave ask.

"Well, I can say that you are one hell of a gentleman, and you're very passionate and considerate. I like that about you a lot, and your not selfish, which is a great thing. I can see us making it official as in relationship soon," Treasure respond.

"Wow, I wasn't expecting to hear that, but hey, I'm ready when- ever you ready no need to feel pressured or rushed about it," Dave said.

"I'm just letting you know in advance so you won't try to slip away from me," while laughing ha, ha, ha, ha Treasure respond

"I'm not letting you go, my dear, you the only woman I see and have my full undivided attention," Dave respond while smiling.

Looking through the review mirror, I can see Darren and Starr right behind us. Making it to our destination, we decide to grab some brunch first. We got a table for four and sat across from each other.

"I'm hungry what's good to eat here," Starr asks nobody in particular while looking over the menu.

"Looking at the menu, some of everything looks good to me," Darren responds.

Darren was dealing with a slight hangover from the night before an outing with Dave, so eating will help him at the moment. At least help him find some type of energy.

"That hangover kicking your ass bro after all," Dave says.

"Yeah, it is no lie, bro, but I once I get this food in me, I will be straight," Darren responds.

"What pool hall did you guys go to if you don't mind me asking?" Treasure asked Dave.

"Oh, we didn't go to a hall; we went to a bar that has a pool area downstairs in the basement," Dave responded.

"Oh, okay, just checking, I didn't want to go to the same hall, that's why I was asking," Treasure respond to Dave.

"If it was, we still would be okay with going out," Dave said.

"Hell yeah, we wouldn't have a problem with it at all, sweetheart," Darren assure both of us.

"I'm ready to order, I don't know about you guys," Starr says.

* * *

Soon after, Starr says that a waiter comes to take our order. We all order big meals and drinks to continue along with our date. The drinks make their way to the table before our meals, and we all take sips of our drinks.

"Alright, let's plan this game of pool out before we get there, we play couple vs. couple for best of three. Then we play you guys vs. us best of three. We can make a beat once we get there," Starr suggests.

"Deal, that sounds like a plan to me I like the way you think," Darren responds. Dave looked over at me to see what my response would be.

"I'm down for whatever let's do it," Treasure said.

"I just hope these bets don't get too outrageous; that's all I'm asking?" Darren says.

"Okay, it's not; we all just have to agree on whatever we bet, though," Starr say.

"I'm down to play; let's make it fun," Dave say.

"Alright, we all agree," we say in unison.

Our meals come to the table and can you say we all made sure to enjoy it. We do a lot of talking amongst each other Darren and

Starr kept us all laughing throughout the out the afternoon. Thinking to myself, maybe it was a thing to actually allow my to bestie on a blind date with Dave's brother, after all. They look as if they're really into each other, I just hope so. Drifting off in my thoughts, my little girl comes to mind. I can't wait to spend time with her and enjoy life with her.

"Treasure, Treasure, tapping her on her shoulders breaking her out of her daydream, Dave calls me.

"Huh, I didn't even hear you calling me my bad, I have a habit of daydreaming sometimes," Treasure says.

"Oh, it's okay, but you were smiling but wasn't saying anything when I called you. I just wanted to see if you would like another drink before we pay the bill," Dave asked.

"Sure, I wouldn't mind having another it won't hurt," Treasure respond.

"Okay, I'll pick it up while I pay the bill, I 'll be right back," Dave assures Treasure. Darren and Dave both got up and walk over to the front register. These guys are some true gentlemen; after all, I can say that much about both of them.

"Girl, I think I have found the one for me after all, he is such a charm and sarcastic like myself," Starr says.

"I'm glad you guys actually click so well. I knew you would find somebody in this world who would meet your personality halfway and be able to accept you for yourself," Treasure said.

"If it wasn't for you meeting your boo thang, I may not have come across him so easily. Are you enjoying yourself, though? I notice you drift off a little not too long ago," Starr asks.

"Oh, yeah, I am actually I'm loving the fact we are able to double date and enjoy it. I just was thinking about baby girl, that's all," Treasure reply.

Changing the subject but assuring Treasure I understand instantly right before the guys walk back to the table with flowers and drinks in hand.

"Oh my God, did you really have to get flowers for us!" Starr squeals.

"It's our way of letting you two know we appreciate spending time with yawl," Dave says.

Reaching over to give Treasure her dozen roses and drink along with a card.

"Thank you so much. I appreciate it," Treasure says.

"Thank you, Darren, for even considering to get me some flowers even though we barely know each other," Starr said.

"Oh, I'm just being a man showing a beautiful woman like you a good time; that's all and keeping you interested," Darren responds.

"Alright, after this drink, I'm ready to go play some pool. I want to start this game of couple vs. couple first," Dave say aloud.

"That's fine with me, we going to beat yawl ass anyway just like I did you last night," Darren says to Dave.

"I'm let you talk tonight, and I'm showing my baby how a boss play and brag differently," Dave say.

"It's cool we will see about that after all," Darren responds, tossing the last of his drink down.

We get up from the table and make our way to the pool hall to finish off our little day of fun. Deciding to take my car off to my home before going to the hall, we head over to my place to leave it. Starr and Darren sit in the back together and entertain each other the entire way to the pool hall.

Arriving at the pool hall was a breeze that didn't take long at all.

Like the gentleman, they are Dave assist me out the car, and Darren does the same for Starr. She just has to be so extra with it; she wouldn't be herself if she didn't. Exiting the car, she take a bow and say, "Oh, my God, where have you been all my life?" Starr asks Darren playfully.

"I don't know, you tell me, queen," Darren responds.

"I can get used to this kind of treatment from a man," Starr says while walking to the door entrance.

Dave reaches for the door and holds it open for us, but letting it go when Darren walks forward.

"You're on your own brother," Dave said while laughing aloud and watching the door slam in Darren's face.

Turning around to see what the fuss was about, Starr and I burst into laughter.

Darren walks inside and catches up to us and slaps Dave in the back of the head.

"Silly ass play too damn much," Darren said to Dave. "Shut up, having fun like the old times doesn't hurt; it's all out of love,

bro," Dave said.

"We will be back, Starr and I go to the bathroom to freshen up and use the restroom," I say to the guys before walking off.

"Okay, we will be at the table getting the drinks and setting the table," Dave say.

* * *

Walking towards the bathroom, Starr says, "Girl, I like them, their true gentleman."

"That is true, I like the brotherly bond they share with each other. We're about to enjoy the rest of our date and reflect on it later," Treasure said. Before getting back to the date, we freshened up. Starr added a touch of lip gloss to her lips, and I fix my hair.

"I'm growing my hair back out, I miss my hair," I say to Starr.

"I really like the short look on you; it fits you," Starr said.

"I know it does; it just goes well with my face structure, but I miss having my back-length hair that I can throw in a bun and go about my way without the worry of if my hair is out of place," I respond.

"I feel you that can be hectic. You should keep it for the summer, though," Starr says before walking out the bathroom.

"Took long enough," Dave says soon as we get to the table.

"Well, you know us women have to do some freshen up," Treasure respond.

"Let's get this game started, Starr says while picking up the pool stick.

"Hold on, sweetheart, we suppose to making a bet on these games," Darren says.

"Yeah, this game is about to be interesting after all," Starr responds.

"Alright, you and Starr come up with bet for us. Treasure and I will come up with a bet for you guys. After that, Starr and Treasure come with a bet for us fellas, and me and bro will come up with one for you beauties, fair?" Dave says.

"Deal, let's start with couples bet first," Darren responds.

"Okay, well, wait to give us a minute to talk it over amongst each other, Starr suggests.

Turning towards our dates, we begin to come up with some bets that we would all agree on.

63

"Okay, time to play, so what's the bet," Dave say.

"Why we have to go first, heads or tails and tails go first," Darren suggests.

"Cool, I got head," Darren say.

Tossing up the quarter, it lands on tails, "Damn man," Darren yells out.

"Alright cool, we bet that if we win, you and Treasure have to go get matching tattoos, and we have to choose it," Darren say.

"Okay, that's cool; we bet that if we win, you and Starr have to go out again on a serious date, and we will babysit but we get to choose the event," Treasure say.

"Okay, cool that isn't nothing, lets play, Starr says.

"Ladies go first," Darren says, allowing Starr and Treasure to start the game off.

"Well, no need to say it again; I'm ready you want to go first, Tray," Starr suggests.

Walking up to the table and picking up her stick and grabbing the chalk to apply to the tip, Treasure gets ready to break the rack.

To my surprise, she made a good break with two stripes going in back to back. Taking the stick from her to go again for us, I end missing the cue ball. "I don't know why you let him take the stick, you were doing good on your own," Darren laughs.

"Shut the up I only miss because I wasn't focused," Dave responded.

"It's no need to explain yourself brother we know I'm a champ at this," Darren say.

Starr grabs a cup and pours herself a drink and position herself to shot. "We playing right or talking shit to each other," She says.

Hitting the cue ball and knocking an all-white ball in with ease.

"Okay, girl, lets play I see I got some competition go on," Treasure responds to Starr.

Giving Darren the stick to go for us, he walks over, puts chalk on the stick, and whispers to Starr, "We gone shot this next shot together, I'm gone guide you," He says.

Starr bends over, taking the stick from my hand, and I guide her to aim this long shot, which would give us a chance to knock in the cue ball and white or two cue balls.

Dave pours a drink into a cup and gives it to me.

"Oh, I see you, hey, do your thang playgirl, Treasure says to Starr.

"We about to have a good time for the rest of the evening, I see," Dave says.

"Yeah, we hit our target, aiming for the right one," Darren say.

"It's cool go head with your bad self, don't miss this time around," Dave say.

Darren lets Starr do her own thing next time around.

Realizing everybody has a drink in hand or nearby, he pours himself a cup.

"I'm ready to play, let me get this drink in my system real quick," Darren says.

Tossing his drink down like it's water, he grabs the pool stick and knocks in two balls.

"Gave me the energy I needed," Darren said while laughing.

"Let's show them how we coming boo," Starr says.

"Don't get too big-headed now," Treasure responds.

"I'm not even gone let these big head high ego eccentric people get to me, the winners always play with ease and comforts," Dave responds.

"I like that in you honey," Treasure say.

Walking towards Dave to get some public affection from him. He gives me this look with this glow in his eyes that reads come here.

Starr goes to play some music, and Cardi B comes on playing through the speakers.

She starts dancing, and I go join my friend to give us some excitement on this day.

Darren scratches and knocks the cue ball in the hole. Dave takes his turn and knocks three in back to back. Leaving us with two balls to knock out plus the eight ball to win game one. Playing the best out of three to give us a fair chance to win. I take the pool stick f rom Dave's hands while dancing to the table seductively giving him the eye, I bend over and knock both balls in with ease. Walking over to me, he slaps my ass and reaches for a kiss. Smiling from ear to ear, I look at Starr.

"Get a room why don't you love birds," Starr says.

"They some straight L7's, it's cool let them shine in their little glory," Darren says.

"We're not no jealous people we gone give credit when it's due," Starr says.

Walking to Darren giving him a high five and laughing.

Treasure whispers to Dave, "Let's take this eight ball together."

Starr pulls out her phone and snaps a pic of Dave and me instantly.

The ball goes in, and with ease, we set up for round two.

"Aye bae, I don't hear the same noise I heard earlier," Dave laughs.

"I don't hear anything no more, but we are gone be generous and let them start round two." Treasure say.

Starr rushes over to crack the rack with no hesitation, "Let me show them who the boss is," She says.

To back herself up, she knocks in three white balls.

"Okay, see, we let yawl win the first round," Darren says.

"If you say so, I let you think that," Dave responds.

Another couple comes downstairs and begins to play a game across from us.

"Hey, watch them play and get some tips and try winning these two rounds," Dave said to Darren.

"Man, I'm good. I don't need to know tips, and nor do I need to watch somebody else to play," Darren say.

Starr walks over to the couple and asks if they would like to join in the next game girls vs. guys.

They agreed, so the game just got even more interesting for us. A good way of really enjoying ourselves after all.

Treasure and I end up losing the pool game for the couples.

It was cool we didn't mind having to get matching tattoos, I just hope its nothing crazy that Darren and Starr agree on.

We took the L, but we had fun and enjoyed ourselves. Getting back to the pool game waiting on the ladies to come up with there bets. We give them some time to think about it, waiting for them. I set up the table.

The ladies come to the table and tell us there bet, to my surprise they didn't come up the same bets, they came up with different bets for each of us, if they were to win.

Starr bet my brother that if he loses, he would have to take her to Victoria Secret on a five hundred and fifty dollar shopping spree. Waiting to hear what Treasure bet is, I hope it's not the same bet, to my surprise it wasn't, Treasure bet to me was that if I lose, I have to take her to the Spa Day of her choice and I have to give her the massage. She gets to choose what spa to attend. Looking at her giving her direct eye contact, I smile and assure her I agree with her bet. The couple that Starr invited to play along with us, she bet that her significant other to take her out to eat red lobster, and take her on a shopping spree of her choice.

This game of pool guys vs. ladies has gotten very interested, us gentlemen have a few good bets to reveal to the ladies. Letting Darren go first, he bet Starr that if she loses, she would have to be open to continue there relationship after today and that she would

have to take him to the next sporting event of his choice. The gentleman that was invited to play he bet his lady to fix him whatever meals he requests for a week straight. I bet Treasure to a night of lovemaking and for her to role-play, but I get to choose the character. The ladies give us all these looks of death. Like they weren't pleased with the bets we made, but hey we're man what else is it to bet on. Smiling at Treasure, she looks at me and licks her lips with ease and takes a sip of her drink. I guess that was her way of letting me know that she agrees with my bet.

We allow the ladies to go first, and Treasure breaks the balls and leads two stripes to go in back to back. Smiling from ear to ear, she gives the stick to the Starr, and Starr cracks one in the hole. She swayed her hips back and forward and gave the stick to the young lady she invited to play along with us. She knocks two balls in instantly, looking over at my brother he wipes his head across his forehead. Treasure laughs aloud catching him, and says, "Don't panic brother; it's just a game of fun and only game one."

"I can't help it, you'll not playing fair, and the game just got started sis," Darren respond.

Starr walks towards Darren and whispers in his ear.

We don't know what it is she said to him, but he immediately started laughing and smiling.

I can tell my brother and Starr will make a good couple for each other. I just hope they can deal with each other after all.

Getting back focused on the game, the girls end up beating us the first game. With two more games to go before determining who would have to go through with the bets. Taking are time in the second game, not rushing or egging each other on, we play with comfort. Sharing a lot of laughter and dancing around, we decided we had enough on the drinks for the evening. After finishing up our second round of pool, we the guys end up winning the second game. Game three was left to determine the winner; the ladies were giving us a go for are money. We end up with two balls on the table plus the cue ball. It was the ladies' turn to go, and with ease, Treasure knocks in the eight ball the only ball they had left and

give them the 2-1 win. Leaving us fellas having to figure out and find some time to complete the bets. With that, we decide to head over to my place and chill for a little bit and watch a few movies downstairs in the basement, and order something to eat just to end our date on good terms for the evening. We end up exchanging numbers with the couple we met at the pool hall. I guess I can see myself doing another couple of dates again. It was filled with laughter and having a good time without the headaches. Leaving the pool hall, we all get in the car and head to my place. Darren and Starr communicate amongst each other the entire ride home.

* * *

Arriving at my place finally, we all exit the car. Allowing the ladies to enter first, Starr gasps at the sight of the front room, "Wow ^{this} interior layout is beautiful, I would think a woman reside here," she states.

"Aw, thank you, but one of my longtime friends did the layout for me; I just gave him the colors and asked for it to be suitable for both male & female. He did quite a good job with it," I respond.

"So what would you like to watch and what would you guys like to eat," I ask.

Waiting on them to decide on it, I go downstairs to my little built in space that I call a man cave. Letting down the projector and setting up the screen. I go to the bar and pour glasses of wine and put some popcorn in the microwave. The ladies soon find there way downstairs.

"This home is beautiful did you have a family in mind when you had it designed," Treasure asked.

"Yes, I did. I set my home up so that I can build a family and be comfortable where I am without having to go find a bigger place," Dave responded.

"Yeah, he has always been like this even as kids optimistic about the future and setting up things before it could happen. See me, I'm the total opposite of him," Darren responds.

"It's nothing wrong with him being optimistic and doing things in that matter. There isn't nothing wrong with living the bachelor's life either," Treasure assure Darren.

"I know, I'm just saying, some woman would look at it differently. Even though its how he been his entire life," Darren responds.

"I actually like that in him; it shows a lot about him," Treasure says.

"Well, that's why you two will be perfect for each other, after all. A man who is considerate about his future is just what you need," Starr says. We eventually had to decide on what movie to watch, not really sure I just put on my prime account and let the ladies choose. Just what I expected, they settled on a drama love story. Deciding to order some pizza while we watch the movie and enjoy the rest of the night. Cuddling with Treasure was something I could get used to. The pizza finally arrives, with the movie being still in the beginning phase.

It was a good movie so far, a drug dealer and his family hustle. "I will be right back, the pizza is here," I excuse myself.

Making my way upstairs to go pick up the pizza. I go look out the window to see if the delivery guy is outside, and there's no sign of him. While looking out the window, what I do notice is a car, it looks like someone is inside. I go outside and walk in the direction of the vehicle, and whomever it is looked up and spends off immediately. I ignore it and go back in the house checking to see if my outside camera caught the view of the car plates or to see if it picked up on how long the person may have been sitting outside.

Being able to catch a glimpse of the license plate first few digits was all the camera caught.

Calling the pizza company to see where the delivery is while pacing back in forwards. I wait for them to answer and give them my address immediately; they let me know the driver should be pulling up in just a few minutes. Looking out the window again and, to my surprise, the same car that speed off after noticing me coming pulling right back up. The driver gets out and looks at me and says, "You scared me, I thought you were trying to rob me, I'm sorry I didn't know you were picking up your order," He replies.

"My fault I didn't mean to scare you at all; it's just rare for a car just to be sitting outside, so I thought you had the wrong address or something," I reply.

Reaching out to shake the driver's hand and apologizing, I hand him a generous tip and take my food. The little incident I had at the club the other night has me on edge, not to mention the car that I noticed outside the restaurant. Getting back in the house, Treasure comes upstairs.

"I was trying to figure out what was taking you so long," She asks.

Scratching my head and looking up at her while locking the door, "Oh, just had to look out for the delivery guy, that's all," I reply.

"Oh, okay just was checking on you, do you need me to help you?" She asks.

"No, thank you, honey, I got it," while making my way downstairs.

Sitting the pizza down along with the paper towel and plates.

"I had to send Treasure upstairs to see what was taking you so long," Darren responds.

"Oh, I was looking out for the delivery guy, I somehow scared him off approaching his car," I respond.

"How you manage to do that?" Darren ask.

"I looked out the window and went outside and walked towards the car, trying to figure out who it was, and he drove off," I respond.

"Oh, damn, that's crazy; he just came back and told you," Darren said.

"Yeah, he came back after I called in to see where is the order," I respond.

Still not ease by the situation that happen, it caused me to ponder on the incident in the night club. Getting up to grab a beer out the fridge, opening the can and drinking it up before I could make it back to the couch, I had to turn around and grab a few more. "Aye, bro here catch," I toss him a beer.

Taking my time to get back into the night. I grab me a slice of pizza and chill under Treasure.

With ease, we got back into the movie and turned out to be a good night after all.

"So, how did you guys like the movie?" Starr asks.

"It was a good movie, after all, I really enjoyed it, even though it wouldn't be something I would pick out on my own to watch," Darren respond.

"It was interested, I like the family hustle and how they stuck with it and kept building on it even though the pressure became too much to deal with," I responded.

"Yeah, it was a good movie. I like how it ended," Treasure responded.

"Well, I'm glad we all enjoyed the movie, it's now time for a sister girl to get home and get some beauty rest," Starr replied.

"I agree with you on that one, I'm tired as well," Treasure agreed.

"I really enjoyed myself tonight throughout the event of activities we had," Darren assured us.

"Well let's get these beauties home so they can get there beauty sleep bro, I enjoyed myself as well today," I respond.

"Alright, I'm ready whenever you are ready, brother," Darren, reply.

With that being said, the ladies head upstairs and start to put on their belongings.

Following behind them, we make our way upstairs as well. Grabbing my keys and waiting for them to come outside. My brother locked up the crib, and he and the ladies make it to the car. On the way home, the ride was quiet to my surprise; looking in the rearview mirror, Darren and Starr both was knocked out sleep. Looking to my right and Treasure is knocked as well.

Arriving at Starr's house since her place was closer, I wake Darren up to let her know we have arrived at her place. Treasure looks up with this bewildered look in her face and looks around, and reply,

"Oh, we made it drop Starr off already, I call her in the morning."

By the time Treasure had awakened, Starr had already entered her home, with Darren behind her.

"Are you alright?" I ask her,

"Sure, I'm okay. Why, you ask?" She replies.

"Just that you had this worried look or look of confusion expression on your face when you woke up," I respond.

Looking out the window, she responds with a barely heard, "Oh, I'm okay."

Leaving it alone, I notice Darren making his way back to the car. Letting him get in, we make our way to drop off Treasure. Approaching the front of her place, a Sliver car comes from next door driveway. I notice it but I really didn't pay any mind to the make and model of the vehicle. Getting out of the car and assisting Treasure out, I walk her to the entrance, and we share a passionate kiss.

"Let me know when you guys have made it home safely. I really enjoyed myself tonight with you and your higher self-centered brother," She says. Chuckling, at her comment about my brother.

"I'm glad you did enjoy yourself and Darren yeah, that's him, after all. I can't complain too much about Starr, she is fun to be

around and just may be able to handle him after all. Anyhow, I will gladly let you know when we make it home safe. Now you get some rest. Lockup and goodnight," I reply.

Walking back to my car, I look back to see if she was looking through her blinds. Not at all, she wasn't in view at all. Thinking to myself, Taking my time to really get to know her is what has me on my toes as far as getting to know her. It's a few things I notice about her that she doesn't speak on a lot about. I plan to break her out of it because I want us to build and feel comfortable to discuss any and everything with each other. Making it back to the car, I get out of my thoughts and make the ride home.

"So what do you think of her bro?", I ask Darren.

"She's perfect for you, I like how you can see the chemistry between you two," Darren said.

"Are you feeling her friend, it seems like you two enjoy each other company," I say.

"Starr, Starr just might be my lucky shooting star; after all, we have been chatting since you gave me her information. After enjoying quality time with her, she is good so far," He responds.

"That's good just take your time to get to know her and trust me you will find out if she's for you," I respond.

Making it home finally, me and bro exit the car and walk in the house and head to our rooms. I text, Treasure we made it home safe and telling her to enjoy the rest of her weekend. Taking a shower before calling it night.

* * *

Treasure

Tonight, was very much worth it, I needed to relax my mind. I was actually glad to see that Starr and Darren actually got alone.

Picking up my phone and noticing that Dave texted me.

Dave: I enjoyed myself tonight.

Me: I did to, I can't wait to see you tomorrow for our one on one date.

Dave: I can't either, I will ttyl.

Me: Ok, goodnight.

Calling Starr instead of waiting to tell the morning, I had to talk to her. Waiting on her to pick up. She does; it's like she was anticipating me to call.

"I was just debating if I want to call you or wait to tell the morning," Starr says.

"I'm glad you answered, girl, while in the car, I had gone to sleep on the way dropping you off, and I had this crazy dream," I say.

"About, what don't tell me it was Trenell crazy ass," She says.

"Yes, it was about him, and in the dream, he was following Dave and I" I reply.

"Oh my god, I think he's looking for his child; that's why," Starr says.

"I hope not. I don't think he knows about her, from what I know he knows is that I got an abortion," I respond.

"Just know I'm there for you, and maybe we need to make our next date

73

out to the gun range after all," Starr says.

"Sure enough, we really do, what's the kicker is that Dave noticed the worried look on my face while in the car and I told him it was nothing," I say.

"Well, you would have to let him know what it is that bothers you and let him know you suffer from anxiety and depression," Starr says.

"Yeah, I do I'm just have to take it one day at a time and find another way of dealing with it, until I can find the strength to explain it all to him," I respond.

"So, what do you think about Darren?" Starr ask.

"Oh, you and he gets along well, he's arrogant and self-centered, but I think its only because he so uses to woman throwing their self at him. The chemistry between you and him so far is great; I think you're going to pull em out of his ways," I reply.

Starr laughs, "I love that your so blunt and honest about shit. I noticed that with him as well we set up my little shopping spree for next week. I will be calling you to let you know how things go. I'm about to call it night, I have to pick up Trinity. I promised mom I would pick her up. Love you girl and relax don't allow the thoughts of Trenell to cause you to lose a good one," She says.

"Okay, what time you going to church I will meet you there?" I ask.

"Service starts at 10 am, I will see you there," She responded.

Hanging up.

Walking into the kitchen to make my nightly cup of tea.

I head into my living room and light my candles to relax my mind.

Deciding to take a nice warm bath to ease my mind so I can have a goodnight's rest. Taking my time to do just that, I go check to make sure my doors are locked.

After checking the locks and making my way to relax in the tub, I go ending my night on a more relaxing note. Making my way to sleep.

Seven

Making My Love

Deciding to do things a little differently. By this being the date that we both address that we are a couple after three and a half months of getting to know each other. I decide we would have a nice romantic paint & dinner date. I thought this would be a great idea. I went out of my way to go purchase arts and craft supplies and dinner. While shopping earlier I came across this idea to make her favorite seafood along with some loaded potatoes and asparagus. Yes, a full course meal with the very same wine she had on are first date. Reaching over to grab my phone, scrolling through my Facebook news feed.

Social media is entertaining, but I only use it for business purposes. I notice Treasure post a status just a few minutes ago it reads, having a date night with mister with a kissy face emoji following behind it. I send her a text.

Me: So, I'm just mister huh.

Treasure: Yes, my mister and the world don't need to know who or nothing else.

I also notice she never used her legal name or post any pics of herself on Facebook. Replying to her text, just be here on time tonight. I begin to set up my front room so things can be perfect when she arrived. I set the table for two and light a heart-shaped cinnamon scented candle in the middle. I set up an area on the floor to have are little paint section. Thinking to myself, *I just want to give this lady the world because she deserves it. Showing her she's worth the lifestyle I have planned for us in the future. A woman as sweet as she is with some much excellence about herself how do you disrespect her. She works and enjoys what she does and is still pursuing an education. What more could I ask for in a woman like her?*

* * *

Focusing back on my event, I continue setting up and find some nice music to play while I prepare dinner and desserts. Deciding to do something quick for desserts, I go with chocolate covered strawberries. Putting the crab legs on first, I do just that and set up a pan for the potatoes. Deciding to just get everything cooking at once, I buttered up the potatoes and put them in the oven. Cracking the window to let a breeze of fresh air in the kitchen, the aroma from the crab legs danced through the house.

While everything was cooking, I decided to take a quick shower. Taking my time getting dressed, trying to kill some time. I put on some gray sweatpants and a fitted crew neck gray t-shirt. Yeah, some lounge around clothes, nothing fancy, the best part about having a date at home. Heading back into the kitchen to finish the meal, I put on my apron and continue to go work. Adding a little more seasoning to the crab legs, I hear the doorbell ring. Making sure everything is on point, I go to answer the door, and there she is standing looking beautiful and dressed comfortably in her jogging suit and sneakers. Perfect for the event, she had a carry on bag with her.

"I'm assuming you have a reason for not answering my phone call, I was calling to let you know I was on my way," she says. I grab her waist, pulling her close to me for a long hug and respond.

"Oh, I set my phone down after I texted you and didn't pick it back up; was busy after that," I respond.

"It sure does smells good in here, and it smells like my favorite, grabbing her mouth in shock as she notices the layout.

"Oh, my gosh, you took your time to set all this up for us," Treasure reply.

"Yes, I surely did I have to make this night special," I respond.

"Did you save something for me to put together, or did you prefer me to just relax?" Treasure ask.

"Give me second; I just want you to relax, matter of fact inside my room there is a master bathroom with another gift waiting for you," directing her towards the bathroom we go.

She broke down in tears of joy; I wasn't prepared for that reaction from her. Helping her off the floor, I held her in my arms and comforted her with ease. I had made her a nice warm bubble bath, with strawberry-scented candles around the sink with champagne glasses sitting nearby. On the bed, I had her some nice lingerie laying out and some comfortable pajamas to lounge around in until we got to the bedroom.

Allowing her to get ready for her bath, I go to the kitchen to check on the food. Preparing our plates, so when she gets out of the bath, she can sit, and we can enjoy are dinner. Turning on some music to set the vibe, I take my time tasting everything to make sure its right before placing it on the table. To my tasting, everything was perfect, not too salty and not too spicy, just right.

After getting that out the way, I go to check up on her and bring her favorite wine, Armand De Brignac Demi-sec Champagne. She lookup smiles, and mouths the words; thank you; I pour her drink and give it to her and let her know I will be back. Taking the chocolate covered strawberries out the refrigerator, I place them on a tray. Melting the butter, for the crab legs, I sprinkle some basil and garlic to give it flavor. Changing the music and heading over to the little area I put together for our paint section. I set up everything on the decision to use the floor instead of standing. Makes it more enjoyable if you ask me. Heading into the kitchen and almost knocking myself out just from the site of Treasure standing in the front room dancing across the floor. To my surprise, she put on the lingerie with a silk kimono robe. Caught up and mesmerized by the

looks of her psychic moving with ease across the carpet. I decided just to watch her and not interrupt her, and she says out of nowhere without looking my way like she felt me starring.

"Come join me," Treasure says while twirling around and giving me direct eye contact.

"Aw, you ain't saying nothing but a word," I respond while making my way to her.

Dancing with her for a brief moment, bringing her close to me to the point, I can feel her chest rise as she breathes in and out. Slowly gliding across the carpet and enjoying the moment, I direct her to the table in the midst of us dancing. Pulling out her chair and dipping her right in it so she can see the lovely meal, I prepared for her. Taking my time to let her see that I cooked her favorite, she smiled from ear to ear. Allowing her to prep her plate and pray over our meal before we devoured every bit of it. Enjoying the meal I had prepared for us throughout the night, we just finished enjoying ourselves.

Removing are plates from the table, and bringing in the desserts, Treasure stops me, "Just bring them over here, I'm ready to paint."

"Okay, give me a second while I get the cup of water for us to use," I say.

"Bring me another cup of champagne, please," Treasure asks?

"I got you, coming right up," I respond.

Ready to get into this painting section with her was the best part of this event, I know she enjoys painting, so why not do things she will enjoy. Bringing her a glass of champagne, along with the cup of water, so we can start this paint section and continue with are romantic dinner alone.

* * *

Allowing her to decide on what it is we should paint, and she asks me to give her a second. She walks off and comes back with her phone in hand with a quote that reads, love is a flame that burns everything other than itself. It is the destruction of all that is false, and the fulfillment of all that is true.

"Define that quote in a picture form, and let's see how this journey of love goes with us," she states.

Picking up her paintbrush and going to work instantly. She really does enjoy painting without thinking she has already started drawing. Distracting her, I put my hand over her canvas, she pushes my hand away, and squeals out stop. Grabbing her by her waist, I begin to place a trail of kisses down her neck with passion in between everyone. She eventually turns face to face towards me, and we stare into each other eyes and embrace each other with a long kiss that leads us into sharing a passionate moment. The kisses get steamy, and to say we end up finding our way to the room. Locking tongues and hands fondling around all over each other. I end up making my way down to her love nectar.

Making a trail of kisses and licking her between her thighs, I flicked my tongue across her pearl. Watching her while pleasuring her with my tongue made my manhood stand at attention. Taking my time to make love to her mentally and physically. I let my tongue play in her yard until she couldn't take it any longer. Giving both her breast equal treatment, I suck, nibbled on both until I made my way back in between her legs. This time she grabbed my head and guided me straight to it. Taking my time to part her lower lips, I use my tongue to spell out my name while seducing her till she climaxed. The work of my tongue when it comes to pleasing a woman I love was like art to me. Everybody couldn't get the pleasure of me being so skilled, but Treasure was worth it, and I planned to make her mine forever. Drifting off to sleep with ease.

* * *

Waking up before she could get out of bed, I decided to prepare her breakfast in bed. Using the chocolate cover strawberries to place with the meal since we didn't eat them yesterday. Deciding to make some waffles, sausages, and eggs with a nice cold glass of orange juice to go with it. Looking for my George Former waffle maker, I

find it on the shelf, washing it off due to it being a little dusty. Plugging it in, while I mix the batter and begin preparing breakfast. I was glad it was the weekend that didn't have to rush to get things done. Using the entire weekend to spend with Treasure was the plan. Putting the batter inside the waffle maker with ease, I close the lid to let it cook. Taking out a skillet to scramble the eggs in. I go to work with the rest of the meal. Taking the waffle out and adding in some more batter to make a few more. Getting breakfast cooked was a breeze. Hoping she would still be sleep once I get back to the room, lucky me she was just turning over. Looking up at me, she smiled and didn't notice the food right away. The aroma floated throw the air, and she gets up stretch and says "What is it you don't like doing for your woman? Breakfast in bed, what a way to start my Saturday morning," she says. Getting out of bed to go to the washroom to take care of her morning hygiene.

"Good morning sunshine, it's nothing that I don't like doing for a woman I want to spend my life with," I respond.

"Where are your clean washcloths, and wow what I statement." She say.

"Look inside that mirror on the wall, the one that's behind you; it's a little closet where I store everything for the bathroom," I say to her.

"Wow, didn't even notice it was a closet behind it," she say.

"Don't take to long I don't want your food to get cold. Let's go to the museum this afternoon and enjoy some artwork. If you don't mind," I suggest.

"Sure, that would be fun, and later we can go to the carnival that's down the street from here," She say.

"Okay, sounds like a plan a great way to spend the weekend," I respond.

"Now let's see what this breakfast in bed is like," She say.

Making her way back into the room and sitting on the bed and reaching for her plate.

"It's only special because I made it, everything I do. I put my all into it. I'm about to go finish up are little paint sections we suppose to enjoyed last night. Smiling and giving her the eye.

"You did do some painting last night, your brushed your tongue across my blank canvas all night and had me as your finish work of art," She teased while stuffing her mouth with a strawberry.

"Lady, you better stop before you don't get to that meal, and I have you crawling up the wall next," I jokingly responded.

"Oh, you know morning sex is the best, they say, why not let's see if your really up for it," She say.

Reaching into my night bag, grabbing the lick me off the liquid that Starr bought for me last week, I grab it without him noticing. Making my way towards him with a strawberry in hand, grabbing him from behind kissing his neck, and he slowly turns towards me with this seductive look of hunger. I place a few drops of the liquid on his neck and begin to lick it off slowly, and he looks at my hand, "What's that you have in your hand?" he says.

Reaching for it, along with the strawberry, I insert it into her mouth and squirt a trail of the liquid down her chest. She gets hot instantly, reaching for her face cuffing her chin in my hand, taking a bite into the strawberry with the juices dripping down my chin, I lick my lips and kiss her passionately. Our tongues intertwine with each other, and I lay her across the carpet and dives right into her love nectar, with no hesitation. Using the last of the liquid lick me off edible, I squirt it right above her navel. Sucking each of her breasts and making sure I lick off every drop of liquid, leaving her body with chills. She looks at me with this pleasuring look in her eyes, and whispers, "I want him," looking down at my manhood that was standing at attention.

I whisper, "You can have him let me finish pleasing you the way I enjoy best," I say. Making my way down to her already wet chocolate cat, I insert my tongue in and out and giving her this extreme orgasm. After satisfying her the way I enjoy. I reach over under my couch and grab my box of condoms, strap it on, and slowly enter her love canal. Feeling like I was in trans, I put in work and made sure I left my mark. She wasn't done yet, which took me by surprise, after making her cum like crazy, I thought she would be in for a nap for a little bit. She gets up to remove the condom, and grabs a paper towel and wipe him off and take him inside her mouth with ease. Sending me into a spell, the orgasm she left me with, had me stuck in place for a few minutes. Putting my right to sleep was where we both ended up.

Waking up, realizing we both knocked out on the dining room floor. I nudge her to see if she would move, and she jumps up. "Oh, I didn't mean to startle you. I just wanted to see if you wanted to get in the bed and finish sleeping," I say.

"It's okay; I just had a bad dream, that's all," She responds.

"I'm up for the day now, let's get this day started I see I put you right to sleep," She says jokingly. "Yeah we took each other by surprise. I'm ready to gct this day going going as well its already 12," I respond.

Helping her off the floor and smacking her ass as she walks away. I pick up my phone to see if I had any messages, and to my surprise, like always, Darren has hit my line several times. Replying to his last text.

Me: I'm good bro, just had a long night with my lady. I will hit you up later we spending the weekend together.

Putting my phone back down and going to the kitchen to get something to drink, she drained the shit out of me. Grabbing a bottle of water for her as well, and to find her in the shower. Allowing her to finish her shower in peace, I go to get my clothes out for the day.

Realizing the vibe we share is amazing, ready to go out and enjoy the rest of the weekend with my love. I couldn't wait to go out and have fun with her and break her from the nightmares that have been bothering her. I'm going to assume it's her past relationship; it must still bother her. Another reason I must be careful with her heart, and repair all the pieces and allow her to see all men aren't the same. Laying across the bed, smiling at the thought of her walking down the aisle and just the site of imaging her being pregnant carrying my child. The thought had me so caught up, I didn't even notice that she came into the room and was watching me.

What got you smiling from ear to ear and not hearing me?"she ask. Getting off the bed and embracing her from behind while she put on her makeup, I smile and say, "Oh, I just was daydreaming about you walking down the aisle. Carrying my child in a beautiful wedding dress, that's all," I respond.

She looks at me and laughs, "Go get in the shower so we can get out of this house," she says.

"Alright, lady, I'm going now, don't interrupt me from my thoughts," I reply.

Walk into the bathroom, turning on the shower, and waiting for a few minutes to make sure the temperature is just right. Letting the waterfall over me, I go back to daydreaming about Treasure again. I find it weird that I keep daydreaming about her, and she's in the next room. Getting out of my thoughts, I finish my shower.

Going into my room, to get dressed, Treasure looks at me and licks her lips, I had to escort her out because if she kept it up, we would be in the house all day. "Hold on before you put me out,"

she snaps a pic, don't worry its for my eyes only. Walking out to the kitchen, she goes in the fridge to get the rest of the chocolate covered strawberries and sits at the island and eats them one by one.

Catching her the mist of eating the strawberries, I snap a pic of her, and she looks so seductive without even being aware of it.

"I got a picture of you looking all sexy over there eating," I say.

"Oh, let me find out we snapping pictures of each other without notice," She says.

"Is you ready to get out of here yet it's going on 1:30 pm; we had a late start, but I guess it was worth it after all," I reply.

"What you mean, you guess," she nudges me with her hip and responds.

"I'm just bullshitting you, it was well worth it just wanted to see your reaction," I say.

Ha, Ha, Ha, she laughs, "let me find out you're trying to go off my reactions, you might not want to do that honey, because I can be the happiest woman in the world and you won't even notice it at times," She say.

"Let's go enjoy some beautiful artwork and rollercoasters," I respond.

Walking out the door, with her in front of me, I lock up, and we take my car. Making our way to the museum first to enjoy some artwork, since we didn't get to finish our own.

Arriving at the museum in no time. Treasure is so amazed by all the artwork, the ones she enjoyed she made a note of what the pictures detailed on a little notepad to create her own version of them. Like most art museums taking pictures isn't allowed. Enjoying ourselves and being caught up into the artwork, we would give our thoughts on every piece we stopped by. This helped us to understand each other views on the same things from a different point of view without causing disputes amongst us. This trip to the museum was interesting; after all, we end up stopping by a photo that showed love. She reads the quote she showed me last night off the top of her head like it was poetry.

"Love is a flame that burns everything other than itself. It is the destruction of all that is false and the fulfillment of all that is true," she says.

"That quote means so much more, but it fits this artwork in a certain way," I reply.

"Well, give me a description of what kind of picture will reflect this quote, Mister," She say.

"Now that's kind of deep detailing, you know, I would actually have to sit and think about a good one for you," I respond.

"Okay, when you figure it out let me know, so I can create a piece of artwork for you, and if we get end up moving in with each other, I will bring both pieces together and hopefully the two can combine, with the quote placed above it," She say.

"That will be dope. I can see it now," I respond.

Leaving the museum, she takes a picture of the outside artwork and statues.

"That was interested the whole trip to the museum, and just to be able to have a conversation throughout the date was even more intriguing to me," She say.

"Well, I'm ready to get you nerves going and see how you deal with these rides at this carnival," I laugh.

"Oh well, this will be fun after all because I'm not a big fan of rides," She say.

"I really like the games that they have at carnivals," I reply.

"Oh, okay, so that means I should be leaving with a few pretty gifts tonight," She replies with a smile as big as a kid who is told they can have candy.

Turning on some music to get us hyped up for some fun. Driving back to the city, traffic wasn't bad getting through. Getting closer to where the carnival is held at, that's where the traffic gets hectic at, we end up maneuvering through it and finding a good parking spot after all.

Helping her out the car like I always do, we lock the doors and make our way to the park. Holding hands like a high school couple, we make our way to get a wrist band for the rides, and the games you had to buy tickets for. We get both the tickets and the wrist band.

Deciding we would play, rock, paper, scissors to figure out which activities we would do first. I wanted to do the rides first, and she wanted to do the games. I just wanted to save the games for the last part so we can eat, chill and go back to my house at the end. She ends up losing, so it was the rides that we choose to go on first. Not sure of what rides to get on first, we both pick this tilt the world inside a Pharaoh. The ride goes back and forwards in the air, but each time it goes further and further in the sky and drops.

Getting in line and waiting to see what the hype is about on this ride. We get on and sits next to each other. The beginning of the ride didn't seem like anything to me; it wasn't until I realized that the further it went up, the drop gets more intense, every time. Treasure was ready to get off the ride after the first drop from the air. It took for me to get to the second drop that made me ready to get off. Trying to keep my composure, I suck in my air and finish the ride; the entire ride Treasure squeezed my wrist. It was funny to me because she's actually gripping my arm like a scared child.

Finally, the ride comes to an end, and we exit, I burst into laughter because the expression on her face, tells it all. Catching her breath, she punches me in the arm and says, "That is the first and last ride I'm getting on."

"Why come on just one more, and you can pick it," I say.

"Okay, it's not going to be as intense as that damn Pharaoh," She says.

"That's fine I just don't the wrist bands to go to waste," I reply.

"Alright, let's go get on that rollercoaster," She say.

Walking in line to get on the rollercoaster ride, we get on, and she actually doesn't panic like she did the first ride. Rollercoasters are a bit more excited and not much to worry about verses the rides suspended in the air. After enjoying that ride, she decided we do the go-carts, and a ride called tilt the cup. Playing go-carts with Treasure was fun, and that damn tilt the cup ride had me feeling like I was going to throw up my insides. She laughed and smiled so much; it made my day even more worth it being there with her.

Making our way through the park to find a game to play that she and I would enjoy. She spots a giant teddy bear that she wants.

"I want that giant teddy bear; let's see if you can win it for me," She request.

"If I can't win it, I would be happy to buy it for you," I reply.

The game was to hit the target with the baseball, three times to win the teddy bear. I give my best shot, and with my luck for today, I end up hitting all three targets and winning her the teddy bear. We make our way to play a few more games, winning a gift from each one. Wanting to eat before we leave the park, we had to go put up the gifts.

Walking to the car, Treasure stop to take pics of all her gifts, and I end up bumping into some dude. Catching this sudden drift of air out of nowhere, I turn to look, and I this guy drops a piece of paper. I go to pick it up, and it reads, Bitch I'm gone catch you one day just mark my words. Looking in the crowd to see if I can spot him but, I couldn't with the crowd of people walking in every direction. Treasure walks over towards me, "Can you take a picture of me with my gifts, I was trying to take a selfie, but I couldn't get the perfect angle," She says.

* * *

Taking her phone and taking a few photos for her and adding a few with me and her together. We make our way to the car to put the gifts up. I toss the piece of paper that I had in my hand. Going back into the park for something to eat and calling it a night.

"I want a funnel cake to go, and just to eat some food," She says.

"Okay, we can just take everything for on the go, so we can get back in," I reply.

Making are orders and heading back to the car to get back to my place before it starts to get crazy outside. Assisting her in the car before getting in the driver seat, making sure she's okay. I get in, and we take the drive back to my place. Soon as we get inside, she rushes to the bathroom, damn near knocking me over.

She yells, out, "My bad, but I had to go I sat in the car drinking all that damn pop and I had to pee before drinking it," she says.

Laughing because realizing if she wouldn't made it in time, she would have pissed on herself.

She comes out and catches me, "Let me find out you realized I almost pissed on myself," she says. Laughing at herself, she goes into the room and picks up her kimono and her pajamas to take a shower. I go to the kitchen and pour us a glass of wine and heat up the food we ordered. I bring it into the room and place it on the nightstand for her. Looking in the drawer to find a pair of pajama pants, I go take a shower in the main bathroom.

"Dave, Dave, Dave, where are you?" she calls out. I forgot to let her know I was taking a shower in the main bathroom.

"I'm in the guest bathroom taking a shower, love," I reply.

She finds her way into the bathroom, "Oh, next time tell me, got me looking for you," She reply.

"My fault, I didn't want to disturb you, that's all. Did you see your meal on the nightstand?" I ask.

"No, I didn't even pay attention to it, I just came out looking for you due to it is so quiet," She says.

"Oh, I usually turn on the music before getting in the shower I guess I can say I'm tired," I respond.

"Honey, that makes the both of us then, I'm about to go eat and find something to watch so we can relax for the night," She says.

Leaving the bathroom, she goes into the room, and I finish my shower. I didn't even notice my penis was standing at attention, yeah tired I am. Thinking to myself, *she noticed it, though.* Getting out the shower and making my way to the room.

"So have you found something to watch, or do I have to find something?" I ask.

"You can find something; I was just trying to finish eating," She replied.

Taking the remote, I scroll through Netflix under action & adventures. After scrolling, I find the movie Extinction. Pressing play so the movie can start, I go get some snacks for us to have and some water. We end up drifting off to sleep with ease and not evening touching the snacks.

Waking up feeling refreshed. Turning over to find Treasure up and out the bed, she has really made herself comfortable after all. I smell food cooking, and there she stands in the kitchen with a cup of tea in hand. Cooking morning breakfast, looking up from sipping her tea,

"Good Morning my sleeping beast, I got up early it's a Sunday thing I do," She says.

"Oh, okay, that's fine; I just woke up and noticed you weren't next to me," I reply.

"Want to go to Church this morning, it would be a pleasure for you to come with me," She says.

"Sure, I don't mind attending Church, do you have a home?" I ask her.

"I don't really have a home Church, but I go to the same church that Starr attends with her family every other Sunday," She replies.

"Oh, okay, just was asking. I have a church home that I grew up attending, haven't really been regularly like I should, but if you don't mind, we can make it apart of our daily life to do so," I assure her.

"Wow, where have you been all my life?" She says aloud, not realizing it until I walk over to her.

"Sometimes, people go through the hardships in life for a reason, and now its time for you to be happy with a man who shares the same views as you in life. God doesn't send what you want in your life when you expect it. My mom use to always say that to me, and I kept that in my daily life." I respond.

"Let's get this meal prepared and start this new journey," She said.

She prepares plates, I leave to take care of my morning hygiene, and take my clothes out for Church.

Heading into the kitchen to enjoy our breakfast together.

"So we will go to the Church; you usually attend with Starr if that's fine with you," I say.

She looks at me and nods her head, yes.

Enjoying the breakfast, she took her time to prepare for us this morning. I get up to wash it down with a cold cup of orange juice.

"Breakfast was on point by the way love; you made sure I had a nice big healthy plate," I say.

"Yeah, I had to treat you with breakfast you made me breakfast yesterday. I like to show the same love given in return, and I'm glad you enjoyed it," She says while walking off to the room.

Making my way to the shower as well so we can get to service on time. We both shower and come out of the bathroom right after each other. She comes out and looks at me and smiles, to the mirror she goes. Deciding to wear some nice slacks and a nice button-down top, nothing too extravagant. She had on her slacks and a nice top as well. Admiring her beauty, I smile and watch her do her makeup, something she really doesn't need at all. She looks up at me, "I see you watching me," She says.

"Oh, I'm just admiring your beauty before, and after the makeup, that's all," I reply.

"Oh I just started wearing makeup after my breakup, I decided I need to change somethings and to hide this mark I have on the side of my cheek," She responds turning to show me the scar.

I walk over to her and get a close up of it and whisper in her ear,

"You're still beautiful, regardless to me." Kissing her scar and walking out.

I had to walk out of the room because I started to get lost in my thoughts, which would cause me to go in a rage. I really dislike that she had to deal with such a lowlife of a man in her past. It bothers me a lot. Reaching for my keys off the keyring, I step outside for some fresh air to control my temper. I pace back in forwards, counting to myself and claiming down. Within twenty minutes of me being outside, she comes out and yells, "She's ready to go."

She placed her things in the trunk of her car, and we take my car to service.

Upon arriving at church to my surprise, I notice my brother's car parked in the lot. Let me find out Darren is really shifting gears. Its a good thing; I'm happy for him.

Walking into service, we find a seat together right before the doors close. Service was great, for it being my first time back in the place of the Lord after a while. I really enjoyed service the word spoken, actually stuck with me throughout the day. Greeting and catching up to Darren and Starr before departing, it was good to see them together.

* * *

Hey, bro, I see you and Starr are really growing on each other," I say. "What up, bro, yeah, she's growing on me; I see you two love birds looking real good," Darren reply.

"Yeah, I told you I plan to make her mine, for real for real," I say.

"Yeah, you did say that bro, but I'm about to get back over to this girl before she goes crazy," Darren laughs. We shake up and hug each other and say our see you later.

Pulling my phone out my pocket, I call Treasure to see where she is and to let her know I will be waiting in the car for her. She picks, up "Oh, I was just saying hi to Darren and was making my way to you," she says.

"Okay, I just wanted to let you know I will be waiting in the car. Take your time, love," I inform her.

"Alright, but I'm ready to go, so I'll be there shortly," she responds.

Hanging up the phone and sitting in the car, thinking about just some of everything. Checking on business to see how the catering event went today. I call Candice to see what was going on; she picks up instantly.

"What's up boss, how are you doing?" She says.

"Hey, there I'm actually doing good, feeling good, enjoyed my weekend. How did the catering event go today? What's the sales looking like?"

"That's good your feeling good, but sales were good today both events needed to stock up twice on drinks, I am going to send you the list of everything," She says.

"Okay, I'm taking care of payroll tonight, so don't worry about it today and make sure you send me to restock list as well. New menus for the spring should be dropped off tomorrow, so we may not open.

Depending on how much we have to rearrange," I reply.

"Okay, I will be in tomorrow afternoon anyhow, so I see you then, but I'm emailing you everything right now." She responds.

"Thanks, baby girl, I see you tomorrow finish enjoying your day," I reply.

"Sure will boss," She say and disconnecting the call.

Treasure finally makes her way to the car, and she smiles.

"So did you like the service?" she asks.

"Yes, I actually enjoyed the service we can make it our home church," I reply.

"Okay, well, next service, we can do a meet and greet and get to know everyone," She responds.

"I'm ready whenever you are," I say.

"Okay, that's fine with me, but I have some last-minute studying to get to at home," She say.

"Okay, let's get out here, I have to do payroll and get stock together for my business just checked in with my assistant to see how things went today," I say.

With that said, I make my way back to my place.

Treasure and I exchange hugs and kisses; I let her know I wouldn't be going anywhere for the rest of the day.

"Call me when you make it home. I really enjoyed my weekend spent with you," I say.

"I will, and I enjoyed every bit of the weekend with you as well," she say while getting her car.

I wait until she pulls out the drive-thru before going inside.

* * *

Deciding I would sit outside on my patio under the sun to get some work done, with a glass of wine. Taking out my MacBook Pro, I go to work and open up my business portfolio, making my sales chart for this month and comparing them to lasts month for are monthly meeting. In the middle of me working on my project, I get a call from Treasure, answering it, "Hey there, honey, I see you made it home safely," I say.

"Yes, I sure did I had to hear your voice decided that I would sit outside on my balcony and do some painting," She respond.

"Oh, wow, that's interesting. I decided to come out on my patio to do some work and enjoy the sunlight and the spring breeze," I reply.

"Great minds think alike," chuckling, she responds.

"True, I will let you get back to your painting. I will call you before I leave out for work tonight," I respond.

"Okay, love, I will be expecting your call; talk to you later," she responds.

"Alright, I won't let you down," I say.

Hanging up and getting back to finishing business and using the rest of the evening to rest before work. I make way back inside and lock up, and turn my alarm on.

8:45 pm that night

The sound of my alarm going off wakes me up. Getting up going straight to the bathroom, I use it and take a shower to wake up. After taking my twenty-minute shower and reflecting on my day, I go to the kitchen. Opening the refrigerator, trying to figure out something quick to cook. I choose not to, deciding I will go to the subway for something to eat before making it work. I use the time I have left just to get some much needed rest. Setting my alarm to 10:25 pm to give me time to refreshing and get dressed. I call Treasure soon as my alarm goes off, and she answers after the first ring. Chatting with her for a few minutes, I make my way to freshen up after we disconnect. Getting ready in good timing, I leave my home on time. Arriving to work with time to spare, I get ready for my night ahead.

Eight

Regular Life

Treasure (*Monday Morning*)

Waking up feeling refreshed after a long weekend of enjoyment. It was time to get back to doing what I love doing. Making my way to the kitchen to make my morning breakfast meal and packing it to go. I take care of my morning hygiene and go to make my daily cup of tea. Picking up my phone, I notice my usual text message from Dave. I respond to his text and go take my shower. Since it was nice out, I decide to wear a pencil skirt and my nice peach blazer that went with it. Keeping my makeup to a bare minimum, going for a more natural look. I take a selfie and send it to Dave, with the caption reading, Thinking of you like always love my natural look, and clicking send. Locking up and leaving out for work.

Dave (Monday Morning)

Making my way to my second place of income. I stop by Starbucks to get my usual cup of coffee. I have to push through with y morning activities at the restaurant. Arriving at the restaurant before Candice, so I can put up the new menus and stock up for the week. So she can go about with her daily tasks with no interruptions. I like to keep my family daily tasks as is with nothing extra added to it. That way, it keeps everything running smoothly and steadily.

Checking the camera's like always, nothing suspicious going on. Stocking everything that could be stocked before the truck come. Going into the office to print out a few things, I notice Candice on the camera pulling into the driveway. She is here early than expected, like always. She gets in and yells,

"Boss man, where you at, I got some good news for you," she yells.

"I'm in the office," I respond back, hoping she able to here me.

"Oh, there you are, you remember that new location you were thinking about setting up at for catering only, I may have found the right area," She say.

Reaching into her purse, she pulls out her phone, and she shows me this nice building with great traffic in and out of the area. It shows a for sale sign in the window, showing me the inside of the place. From what it looks like picture-wise, it looks decent. "I'm going to assume you already talk to the owner of the spot, because you got pictures of the inside," I inquire.

"You already know I did my research," She responds.

"Did you get the owner's information?" I ask.

Reaching inside her work bag, she pulls a business card.

"Here you go, I just came from viewing it," She says while giving me the card.

Putting it on my to-do list for tomorrow to call her. Thinking about, Treasure I almost forgot that I had planned to take her to Jamaica after we made it official. I put in order to send her a banquet of roses and edible arrangements with a card that reads; I hope you have your passport we're taking flight next week. Along with the card and roses, I decided I would cash app her some money to go shopping with for the trip. I want to give her the world and show her its more to life when you fall in love. So she can see she found someone who loves and admire the person she is. In the notes for the cash app sending order, I put in Hey beautiful this is for you to get everything you may need for the next surprise I have set up for you.

Requesting for the order to be dropped off tomorrow morning after ten. I get back to work after I have that all done. Waiting on the truck to arrive, I go fill up the timesheets. To keep track of hours I have the team clock in and out both ways paper and digital to make sure we don't miss anybody punches. Looking for Candice to what she was doing, I find her stocking up the restroom supplies.

"Hey there baby girl, after I unload the truck and put up the new menus, I'm getting out your way, let me know if you need anything before I leave," I say to her.

"Okay, I will," she reply.

Looking out the window, the truck pulls up, putting on my back brace I meet the driver out in the back.

Greeting him like always, I open the stock room for easy access so I can get in and out.

"Hey, there, how is it going, I see you're making big progress, I will have to bring my lady up here one night to show support," the truck driver says to me.

"Sure, I would appreciate all the support, I promise my team will make sure you're satisfied from entering to leaving," I reply.

"All is love, homie," he reaches out to shake my hand.

Introducing myself and exchanging numbers, I unload and finish up a stocking. Letting Candice know, I'm out for the night after setting up the new menus she locks up behind me. I go to the gym to let off some steam and chill for the day.

* * *

Treasure

Later during the day

Work was going by smooth; I had decided to take my lunch break a little later. Just to get some extra work done. Checking my phone before clocking out for lunch, and it's a cash app notification. Opening it up and to my surprise, it's a fairly large amount sent

from Dave, reading the note it reads, Hey beautiful use these funds to go shopping, I have a huge surprise for you next week. Make sure you get swim wear, you will need it. Love truly. I smile with excitement, not knowing what this man has up his sleeve. I send him a thank you text and let him know I will go shopping tomorrow after work.

This man has literally made my day even better. Deciding to skip lunch, I call Starr to see if she took her break yet.

"Hey, stranger, how you been?" She answers.

"Stranger, really you have been missing in action. I was trying to see if you took your lunch break yet?" I ask.

"What, damn, I haven't even paid attention to the time I haven't," She responded.

"Well, that's good, meet me at the Nail Bar down the street, Pedi, and Mani on me," I hang up.

Turning on my music and putting my sunglasses on. I make my down the street to the nail bar.

Walking in and like I expected empty, it was. A reserved nice black-owned salon who excepts walk-ins. The owner greets me, and I let her know I will be paying for two both Pedi and Mani's.

"I'm waiting for my friend to come, she should be on her way," I say to the owner.

"Oh, okay, I'm just going to set up for you guys," the owner responded.

Looking out the window, I see Starr on her phone walking to the shop.

Thinking to myself, She looks like she's in a good mood as well, needing to spend some quality time with each other. After a long weekend of not contacting each other due to the sudden life change.

She walks in and smiles and disconnects her phone call.

"I feel so good today, don't know if it's the weather outside or if it's just the affect them Smith's leave on a woman," She says.

"Hey, now maybe it's both I can relate," I reply.

"So you ready to spill the tea because your glowing like a Christmas tree," She says.

Walking over to the pedicure chairs, we take a seat next to each other. Turning the chair vibrations on the desired speed to get comfortable. I take out my phone and begin to show Starr the few pictures of how I spent my weekend.

Looking through the pictures, she say, "You look so happy," Starr says while scrolling through them.

"I feel happy, and love the feeling," I reply.

"I'm so glad you're finally moving forward with life, bestie," She reply.

"This weekend spent with him help me realize I can't keep allowing my fears of yesterday to keep me from enjoying life," I say.

"Well, that's a good thing, and I was surprised to see you both in service yesterday, how did that happen?", She ask.

"Oh, my idea to go to service but his idea to go to the Church that I usually attend," I respond.

"Well, Darren and I didn't spend the weekend with each other, just a day," Starr says.

"That's good, so now what does mom think of him?", I ask.

"Oh, she likes him, she loves that he is educated, and Trinity girl she say he's nice," Starr says.

"That's good, why Dave send me an unfairly large amount of money today and leaves a note that says go shopping and be sure to get swimsuits and that I will need it for the surprise he has scheduled for next week," I say.

"What, you mean when you say he sent a fairly large amount of money, like how much?" She ask.

Showing her my cash app deposit that I haven't even bothered to touch. Her eyes light up, and the first thing that comes out her mouth is, "Girl, you better find some sexy shit, and whatever it is, he got planned yawl gone have some fun," She say.

"It sometimes feels like a dream to have a man like him to enter my life after all the hectic I been through before," I say.

"It's gone feel like that for a while, you just have to get used to it," Starr says.

"Not really knowing how to adjust to all of it, I just pray that it doesn't drift away," I tell Starr.

"Oh, don't worry about that, he is real man, and he knows what he wants he went searching for you," She chuckles and say.

"Not to be in yawl conversation, but it sounds like you have found you, good man. Your friend is right; he is not going anywhere unless you push him away," The owner says.

Taking the advice of these ladies, I smile with ease and continue to enjoy my mini spa.

"Would you ladies like a glass of wine or mimosa?" the owner asks. "Wine," we both respond in unison.

Coming back with two glasses of wine and an assistant, she goes to work on my pedicure. Using some gel-like heat that relaxes me and leaves my feet feeling smooth, I reach into my purse and gives her a tip because her service was just that good. Walking over to the table to get my nails done a much-needed refill, I get my usual ombre set. Starr gets her bright colors like always. Realizing that time has gone by so fast, I have twenty minutes to get back to work. Paying for the service, I kiss Starr and let her know I'm going back to work and I will call her later. She thanks me for treating her out, and I feel this positive vibe over me after leaving the shop, I make my way back to work and decide to order in.

Picking up my phone, and there's a text from Dave, it reads, Joy comes when you allow the sun to shine even when it rains. I told you I got you, and I mean that making you happy is apart from my daily task. Texting him back, I respond Thanks for wanting to be

my sunshine when it rains; I will allow you to be my joy in life daily.

Getting back to work with a smile on my face, I use the rest of

the day to keep my spirits up. Not allowing anything to knock me off my cloud. Thinking of my favorite quote deciding when I get home to create my two pieces of artwork for them. To keep my week going and continuing the positive vibe. Moving on with my day at work and now anxious to get home. I send him a text saying; I would talk to him later, putting my phone up for the remainder of the day.

Finally, getting off work and making my way home. I kick my shoes off soon as I get in the house with no hesitation. Making my way to my room to find me some lounge around the house clothes to wear and paint in, finding just what I needed my t-shirt I use to paint and a nice pair of sweat pants. I go to my kitchen to prepare my cup of tea and light my candles in my living room. Creating my mood so I can continue with my relaxing day. I go run my shower and take a quick ten-minute shower. Anxious to start painting something, I know that I want to be finished until the end of the week because I like to take my time with my artwork. My stomach growling is what disturbs me from my section. I go into my kitchen to fix me something to eat and end up turning the TV on and falling asleep on my couch with ease.

Waking up hearing the birds chirping, not realizing, I slept through the night. Picking up my phone to check the time, three hours before its time for me to get up. With that being said, I decided to make a run for about an hour. Wanting to keep the same energy I started off with yesterday, doing something to keep me feeling good was the way to go. Making it out of the house to exercise after

having a small breakfast. I put my headphones in my ear, and strap my phone on my wrist and take my first lap. Knocking out three laps before calling it enough, and heading back in the house to get ready for work. Taking a shower after sweating out my pours and get ready for a beautiful day at work.

Thinking about, *what Dave could have up his sleeve, after all. For him to send me such a large amount of money, must be a trip. Remembering, I have to go shopping after I get off work was my plan for today after work.* I prepare myself another small breakfast meal to pack with me for work. Locking up and setting my alarm, I make my way out.

Trenell creeps up and instantly deactivates her alarm system. Creeping in the thru the balcony doorway while she was on her run. He hides in the closet the entire time until she leaves. Going through her computer, he finds out the information he been looking for. Coming across the email about the adoption of his daughter that she lied and told my family he aborted. Sneaky bitch, now I'm really about to make her life hell. Leaving the same way, he came in out the balcony he leaves

Getting to work with ease, checking my phone, I notice Dave texted me.

Waiting until I got to my office to respond to him. I get upstairs to my office and text him back right before I get into my work. Taking my time to get started, this eerie feeling comes over me; I ignore it. Using the rest of my day to think positive and stay focus on what's ahead. Deciding to call Starr, before my break to see is she going on lunch now. As usual, we meet up during our lunch break to have a chat about whatever and everything. Grabbing something to eat at Panda Express for lunch something that is light on the stomach. Dave texts me it reads, Hey there; you have a gift waiting for you at the front desk. Let me know when you get it; I hope you like it. Smiling after reading his message, and Starr catches me, "What got you cheesing like a fat kid that ate a piece of chocolate cake?"

"Oh, just Dave, always up to something he got me another gift waiting at the front desk," I respond.

"You know I have to be noisy, so be sure to tell me," She say.

"I will let you know for sure; I'm anxious to see what it is. I plan on getting off an hour early today, so I'm ending my lunch a little early," I respond.

"Okay, girl that's fine with me, just call me after you get home, I have to see what you pick up," Starr responded.

"You know I am, but I will call you, girl, I'm about to make my way back to work," I say.

"Okay, call me," Starr says.

Gathering what I have left of my lunch, I get ready to leave. Putting on my sunglasses and running my fingers through my hair, I walk back to work. Making it back to work, the receptionist stops me, "Hi, Treasure here is a gift that was sent for you," the receptionist says to me.

"Thank you," I respond and reaching for the gift.

A banquet of roses and edible arrangements, and a card. Opening up the card it reads, Hi beautiful I hope you have your passport because we're taking flight next week. Grabbing my mouth to keep myself from squealing so loud. I walk towards the elevator with

tears of joy filling my eyes. Making it to my office I call Starr, she picks up instantly, "Let me call you right back, Treasure." She disconnects, and I go to call Dave, and he doesn't answer, so I shoot him text message.

100

Really now just anxious to leave and go shopping today, I go about the rest of my work week and put in a request for a vacation. That way, whatever it is, he has planned my work schedule won't get in the way. This man has giving and showed me so much love since

the very first day of meeting him.

The rest of my day go by with ease, finally making it home after shopping. I notice my alarm doesn't alert upon entering my home. Not wanting to jump to assumptions, I just assume I didn't hit set after putting in the code. Tossing my new clothes on my sofa and making my way to turn on my music to prepare for next week's surprise. Singing along to Halsey - Now or Never. Picking up my phone, not even hearing it go off. Realizing that Dave has called me twice and sent four text messages. Returning his call, he answers on the first ring.

"Hey there, love how you're doing did you receive your gift," He asks.

"Yes, I was calling you earlier today to let you know I did," I respond.

"Oh, okay, just making sure, but how was your day," He asks.

"I can say my day has been good, and the gift made it better because I wasn't expecting it," I respond

"That's good to know; just enjoy the rest of your week, and I will be sure to call you, just be ready Sunday morning," He says.

"Okay, but wait, where are we going if you don't mind me asking?" I ask.

"Don't worry about that; you will find out before we board the plane. I'm about to get some rest and get ready for work later today, dear. Just know that you're in good care, and will enjoy every bit of it," He responds. "Okay, I will talk to you later, get your rest," I say.

Disconnecting are call and not really liking the waiting game that he have me playing. I guess I will have to wait and see, after all.

Nine

Fun on the Island (Jamaica)

❧

Treasure

Excited to be spending quality time away from home and work. Making it to the airport, and we get to baggage claim to check-in are luggage. In the midst of me going to the bathroom and coming back, he pulls out two tickets to Jamaica. Something I really wasn't expecting but happy to be going. Before getting ready to board the plane, we go grab a few drinks and some snacks. These past few months have been extraordinary to spend it with him. He has made me feel good in so many ways. He has made me feel like a virgin all over again; during sex, this man has given me the most intense and everlasting orgasms ever. It's not just that one time during sex, either it's every time we make love. The chemistry we share is unexplainable; just thinking about us makes me smile.

Dave

Catching Tre smiling from ear to ear, I took a picture of her. A habit we both picked up once we got comfortable and really committed ourselves to each other. Tre drifts off to

sleep while waiting to board the plane. I decided to do a last-minute check on my business to see how things going. Once I board this plane, I'm not checking anything until we land back home. This trip is for Tre and I to just setback, relax, and enjoy quality time with each other. Celebrating our six month anniversary. I just want to show her a good time. I had a list of things we would do while there. A little bit of what

I planned for us to do. The first day is spent indoor inside the resort

having a romantic couple spa treatment, just for relaxation after a long plane ride. It will be well needed but, the next day Dunn's river falls and dolphin cove. I hope she's not afraid of dolphins. Yeah, I got it all planned out for us these next five days I plan to enjoy every bit of it. Our last night, I had it all planned out with her favorite seafood. Dinner on the beach resort w/ her favorite wine and music. Just thinking five days just her and me to spend with each other. Sharing our thoughts and getting to know and understand each other more. A smile creeps across my face, just thinking about it.

Checking on my brother before taking flight, I'm so glad my brother has found interest in Starr, it's crazy because they're so alike personality-wise. I shoot him a text to see how he is doing and how things going with him and Starr after all this time. Just to think about three months ago, my brother was talking about me being a softie, and I notice him picking up those same traits. I'm glad that he finally found someone who fits him. He texts me saying he is good and to enjoy myself on the trip.

Waking Tre up before its time to board the plane.She gets up and smiles, "I'm ready for this adventure is it time to board," She says. "In the next twenty minutes, it will be time to board; the plane been here for about an hour," I say, looking out the window.

"Okay, that's even better, no delayed flight, a good way to start our trip," She say.

The flight wasn't too bad an eleven-hour flight to get there, with one stop. I plan to sleep after getting in the air. That way, by the time we land, I will be well-rested and ready to enjoy this adventurous five-day getaway.

Day One Jamaica

Upon arriving in Jamaica, the scenery was amazing. Falling in love with just the view from our room, it was breathtaking. Being able to enjoy this moment and spend it with someone I adore and plan to have a future with makes it even better.

"Hey there love, how do you like it so far?" I ask her.

"This view is just breathtaking, I can sit right on this balcony and paint for days. I love it," She says.

"I'm glad I am able to explore this trip with you, and just so you know, I have something planned for our entire five days here," I say.

"Oh, wow, I can't wait to start exploring and enjoying all of it," She says.

"Well, with that being said, let's start, I have us a romantic spa day scheduled for us in two hours," I say.

"What really, this already starting to be the best time of my life," She responds.

Heading into are suite bathroom, which took her breath away, she was just amazed by it. A his and her sink with a huge walk in shower with the removing shower head, and across from there was the Jacuzzi large tub in a separate side of the bathroom. I was shocked to see such a huge bathroom. Standing in the bathroom, admiring us from the mirror, I bring her closer into my arms. Tilting her head, I place passionate, sweet kisses down her neck and begin to run my tongue down her blouse. Removing her shirt with ease, I take her breast into my mouth one by one, giving them both attention. Dropping to my knees and under her skirt, I go downtown to give her pussy some much needed undivided attention. Not wanting her to lose her balance, I stop and lay a towel across the bathroom floor and assist her with laying down. I go back to pleasing my lady love nest, flicking my tongue across her pearl, spelling out the words I love you, and with every twirl across her pearl, she would moan with pleasure.

After satisfying her, I get up and turn the shower on for her and help her out of her clothes and let her have her peace. Bringing her body wash and robe to her. She looks at me and smiles, and says "Thank you." It's something about her eyes that captivates me; I find myself lost with every stare. Taking my time to freshen up myself while she showered, I prepare myself to do the same once she gets out.

Really ready to get this relaxation moment going with this spa treatment, the long plane ride to get here left my neck all crapped up and my backache. It wasn't enough leg wrong for me; my tall ass needed to reserve a private setting with legroom. By it being a last-minute reservation, I took whatever it was they had to offer. Today was just gone be more of a chill day for us because I know she was tired, she slept through the entire flight. So using this day as a spa date was perfect to just rest.

Making our way downstairs to the resort area and grabbing a drink. After, receiving are drinks, we go to the salon to check-in for are romantic spa date. Waiting to be escorted to the changing area, the receptionists guide us to our private area. Removing are clothes and exchanging to there disposable bottoms; we both ease into the bath. The water was nice and warm and filled with rose petals, noticing there was our welcome kit with champagne and two flutes and chocolate covered strawberries. Treasure makes her way towards me and kisses me gently, "You go out your way to please me all the time, I don't know how or what to do to show you I appreciate all of," she says.

* * *

Just keep being you is the way you can show me you appreciate and let me in your heart is the only gift I ever want from you," I respond. "I will just bare with me in due time, I promise you," She says. I grab her chin and plant a huge kiss on her cheek. Picking up the wine, I pour both of us a cup, and we make a toast celebrating us making it this far with each other and hopefully a lot more. Two lady masseuses comes in to give us are upper body massage. After, the upper body massage, we got out the best part of the massage. The part I was waiting on the full body massage, which turned out to be very relaxing. After this, I, scheduled for us to get manicures and pedicures. Treasure smiled throughout the day, seeing her smile is what kept my day going. She doesn't know that I planned for us to have a romantic dinner upstairs waiting for us once we got back to the room for the night.

Planning to make sweet passionate love to her until we both past out. I had to somehow go back to the room, so letting her spend time to get her nails and feet done, I made my way back upstairs.

Setting up the role-play outfits I had purchased, this is going to exiting. I was going to be her private stripper for tonight and complete all her fantasies.

Getting back downstairs to her, she asks, "Where you sneak off too?" "Oh, just to the restroom and to go do something," I respond.

"Oh, okay, what color do you think I should get?" She asks.

"Whatever color you like, but red will go perfect for tonight's plans," I respond.

"What do you have planned?" She ask.

"I can't tell you; you will see once we're done here," I say.

"You and these surprises, I don't know if I can take any more of them without a breakdown," She respond.

"That's fine with me tonight is different, I say.

Turning to get her nails done, she snaps a picture of me.

"You and your pictures, I see you really enjoy taking pictures," I say.

"Moments of fun should be captured and left with a picture to keep the memory alive," She say.

Smiling with ease because she's like the spark to my flame and the sun to my life on a rainy day.

Getting up and going to the register, I pay for her manicure and pedicure. Now I just have to sit here and play the waiting game. Deciding I would face time my brother up to see how he's doing. He answered on the first ring.

"What's up bro, how is your trip going so far with your queen?" He asks.

"So far, lovely, I'm just waiting to actually get to enjoy it and explore," I respond.

"Okay, I know you probably chilling for today since yawl had that long-ass flight," He say.

"You know me, but tonight so of the fun begins, you know what I'm talking about," I say, chuckling.

Treasure looks over at me because she heard me, and I blow her a kiss.

"Oh yeah, yeah, I know what you on get it in why don't you," He responds.

"I am bro; she doesn't even know what's coming these next few days. I got it planned all out, I be sure to take pictures to share and grab you a few souvenirs," I say.

"Okay, cool, that would be good, but bro, we have to plan a couple's date for about a week to go out there in the future," He say.

That sounds like a plan; we can do that for sure," I respond. "I'm going to let you get back to enjoying yourself. I'm about to get back to work. Glad you called to let me know how it's going. I will see you when you return, bro," He say.

"Alright bro I will let you get back to work, love you," I say.

We disconnect.

I look up, and Treasure is giving me the stare out of hell. I walking over to her, "It was just Darren and that he was asking about the trip, that's all," I explain.

"Oh, okay, tell me something, she says.

I laugh at her crazy self because her mind was in the wrong place. Kissing her forehead, I say "Lady, you are a handful, I see."

"Not really, I just was trying to figure out what it is you can't for that happen tonight." She says.

"Oh, don't worry you will find out," I reply to her.

She gets up from getting her nails done and go sets at the drying table; I follow behind her to sit with her. Admiring her beauty, I can actually see myself falling in love with this lady. This is the most I have ever done for any woman. That's why I know for a fact I will be asking her for her hand in marriage one day. I really wasn't trying to go to the room as of yet, deciding to do a little shopping inside the resort to kill some time. That way, by the time we get done, dinner would be served to the room already, along with the surprise that I have waiting for her.

Picking up some matching shirts that we plan to wear out tomorrow. Getting some souvenirs to take home, along the way. It was time to head back to the room and begin tonight's activities.

Checking with her to see if she was ready to go back to the room.

"Yes, I'm ready if you are," she says.

"Okay, but first I will need for you to put on this blindfold after we get off the elevator," I say.

"Alright, I can do that," She say.

Getting into the elevator together, we make our way upstairs are room. Soon as we get take a step off the elevator, I place the blindfold over her face. Holding her hand and guiding her to the room and allowing her to remove her blindfold after

realizing we have made it inside. She bursts in tears; I had balloons and roses placed all over the room with a gourmet meal.

She hugs me, and with tears of joy in her eyes, she kisses me and whispers, "Thank you, I appreciate all that you have done for me."

"Your welcome, dear. I hope your hungry because I have a gourmet meal in the room waiting for us," I say.

She walks in the room, and there she finds her gifts a Pandora charm bracelet with a heart-shaped pendant, along with matching earrings. She goes to have a seat to see what meal was prepared for us. I had the kitchen prepare us a scallop shrimp with asparagus and lobster tails. She waits on me to sit with her, but I tell her to give me a second. I go into the bathroom and put on a role-playing surprise for her. I come out of the bathroom with my red socks, red silk briefs, and a red bow tie, and I hit the music on a key before exiting the bathroom. She has this huge Kool-Aid smile on her face. She reaches for her wallets, and she pulls out some dollars. Laughing because she's going along with the role too well, she starts tossing dollars. I had to tell her to hold on to the dollars we have to eat.

After eating our meal, I continue with our role-playing for the night. Picking her up and sitting here at the edge of the bed. I go into an acting mode, playing Chris Brown four play I flexed and did all types of moves. It wasn't until I picked up the whipped cream when things got really hot, I think I had her wetter than she expected with all the teasing. Lowering myself on her with the whipped cream in hand, I turn on some Trey Songz. I help her remove her clothes and spray whip cream on her breasts and on the top of pussy and placing a strawberry on top. I lick every bit of it, eat off, and dive in with my tongue to give her the action she was really waiting for. She takes over and makes her way to spray the remainder of the whipped cream on my penis. Licked and sucked every bit of it off with ease.

* * *

Her sex was hypnotizing, and she eases him inside her wet warm love canal. That took me over the top, just to feel are bodies connecting in another way. I lift her on to the bed and take over, pounding her with ease and passion, making sure she feels every inch of me. With every thrust, she would dig her nails into my back, and before you know it, I found myself releasing. Falling asleep with ease for the night, I smile because I surprised myself with performance I put on for her tonight. Drifting off to sleep with her in my arms, I kiss her and whisper I love you. Knowing she was already knocked out for the night.

Day Two (Dunn River)

Waking up to the sun beaming right through the window, I wake her to have breakfast outside on the

balcony. She wakes up with ease, smiles, and says "Good morning.

"Good morning, dear, look like you were sleeping peacefully," I say.

"I was, I don't even recall dosing off, I remember laying in your arms," She says.

"I looked at you and noticed you were knocked out like a baby. Are you hungry? If so, I have breakfast coming up to the balcony in a few minutes." I say.

"Sure, I'm hungry and let me freshen up and put on something appropriate, and I will meet you out there," She say.

Making her way out to the balcony right after breakfast was served, she was looking beautiful even though her hair was tied up, she was even more beautiful with the sun glowing directly on her.

Saying her prayers before eating like she always does, she asks "What is it do you have planned for us today?"

"Oh, today after lunch, we will be heading over to Dunn's fall river, and after that, we will be swimming with dolphins if we have the energy. So you will need your swimsuit today," I say.

"Wow, this is going to be interesting after all," She say. Eating breakfast and sitting outside, laughing and talking having a good time until it was time to get ready. We take pictures of the lovely view, and us together.

Getting ready to go the Dunn's fall river and taking the beach route there, which made it even more adventures. We took pictures throughout the wall climb and had so much fun. The view from the top was so beautiful once we made it. Taking time to capture every moment of being there. They take personal pictures as well, so we ordered them to go, for keepsakes. After Dunn's river fall climb we decided to use tomorrow to swimming the dolphins instead. That little adventure took a lot of energy out of us. So we decided to go outside and enjoy the sunset at the resort, that's what we did for the rest of the day.

Enjoying the sunset and sipping on Margarita's for the night we, use the rest of the night to chill and watch movies.

Day Three (Montego Bay with Dolphins)

So today would be the day we go swimming with dolphins for the evening fun. Having breakfast downstairs in the lobby, we enjoy it. Deciding to go take a swim on the beach and enjoy the morning sun. She steps in the water first, and I just admire her beauty, she looked so amazing in the one-piece swimsuit and cover-up that she chooses to wear. Taking my phone out of my pocket before joining her in the water, I snap a few pictures of her. She notices and turns it into a mini photoshoot, capturing some beautiful pictures of her in the water. She asks me to join her and take some with her. Being able only to capture half photos of us in the water together, we take a few. I get out the water and place my phone on the lawn chair we had brought while there. Sneaky up on her while in the water, I pick her up from behind and dip her in the water. She screams, "Why would you do that?"

* * *

I help her up, and she shoves me into the water, and we play in the water like big kids. Enjoying every moment of it. I don't know what it was, but it's like the inner kid in us came out. I end up carrying her out the water and onto the sand.

"Lets race to the room last one there is a rotten egg," She yells while running off in the sand. Laughing while running and looking back to see if I was coming. Catching up to her before she can even get halfway there, I pick her up and swing around, the smile on her face sends this light of joy to my heart. Just to see her filled with laughter, was a moment captured in my heart.

Finally, making it back to the room, we get ready to head to Montego Bay to swim with the dolphins. The drive to Montego Bay was very short, and we got there in no time. The view was brilliant, taking pictures of the dolphins that were jumping in the air from out the water. We met up with the tour guide and got the rest of our day going.

"Oh my god, I'm nervous," Treasure says.

"Don't worry, I got you," I respond.

First, we were taught how to interact with the dolphins and get friendly with them. It was time to actually swim with the dolphins, holding on to the dolphins they take off in the water. From diving underneath and to ending it with jumping out the water, and racing back to the tour guide. Having the tour guide record us as we took one last swim with the dolphins before leaving. The dolphins were so friendly and before we left they splashed us with water there way of saying goodbye. Deciding to explore Montego Bay, we go to Jerky's Bar & Grill restaurant. The food was good before going back to the resort; we decided to take a walk on the beach and watch the sunset.

* * *

After a long day of fun, we take a long hot steamy shower together. That ends up with us tangled in each other arms. Another night of lovemaking but find are way out to the balcony under the stars with sounds of the water washing against the shore and the stars shining brightly. We make love right under stars; it was intense romantic and different.

Making our way back into the room, we continue to make love before ending our night. Just like every other night, sleep came peacefully. With her laying in my arms, I didn't toss or turn in my sleep, not once.

Day Four Horseback riding & swimming

I don't know what it is about being here in Jamaica, but the time spent in the water was very relaxing. Today we would go horseback riding in the Caribbean waves, all the way to the ranch. We get up and start our morning by making love the early morning. I don't know what it is with this lady, but my sex drive has increased since being with her. She takes over, and I let her be my morning dominatrix. She had me begging to feel her insides when she got done teasing me and making my dick rock hard. Without a doubt, I get what I asked for, and she damn near put me to bed. Having to find the energy, I order a light meal to eat, from room service.

Getting up, she asks, "Are we going out today or spending a day inside?"

"Oh, we're going out the lady I told you, every day I have something planned for us," I say.

"Oh, okay, just checking," she says while walking off.

I walk up behind her and slaps her ass and tell her to get ready.

* * *

Walking to the balcony, I go out to get some fresh air. Going through social media, just to see what was going on. I run across an unknown friend request, ignoring it. I go back into the room to take my clothes out for the day. She comes out the bathroom looking drop-dead gorgeous in this two-piece swimsuit that had a wrap-around like I skirt open for me to view. Walking up to her and kissing her passionately, I had to stop myself because, at the moment, I was ready to devour her like a freshly cooked shrimp meal. "Lady, you better stop, before we end up in this room all night," I say.

"I didn't do anything but be me; I can't help you can't keep your hand off me," She swats my hands away and nudges me into the bathroom. That was her way of telling me to get ready.

Making my way into the bathroom to get ready, I do just that. Taking about twenty minutes to shower and get ready. Coming out of the bathroom in my swim trunks and white beater fitted top. She says, "So I guess I did put on the right outfit today after all," Treasure said.

"Oh yeah, you put on the right outfit for the perfect event," I assure her.

She walks to the floor mirror, and I walk behind her and take pictures of us together.

We make each other look good, "You're ready to go finish exploring the island?" I ask her.

"Yea I'm ready handsome, she laughs after responding to him in Rasta language.

"What did you say?" I ask her. She laughs, and we make our way out the door.

"Oh, you speak Rasta I didn't no that," I say.

"Yeah, I know a little of it, I listen to some of the music," She say.

"Oh snaps, I want you to say something sexy in Rasta," I joke around with her.

"Tonight I'm gaan suck, di soul, outta yuh," She says and smiles.

"I know exactly what you just said, you better stop," I say.

Making our way to Montego Bay stable.

Treasure looks and realizes what it is we will be doing today. "This is going to be so fun, to go horseback riding and swimming in the Caribbean," She says.

Waiting on the tour guide to come out and he comes out with this beautiful black stallion, to give us a brief lesson.

"Have you guys rode a horse before?" the tour guide asks.

"I have not this will be my first time," I respond.

"No, I use to ride horses for fun as a kid up until I became a teenager," Treasure says.

Whispering in her ear, jokingly, I say, "That's why you know how to ride this pipe of mine so good," I laugh and say. She burst into laughter and starts blushing. I love to see her smile. "I didn't know that," I say.

113

"Oh, yeah, well, I did," I say after nudging him for his sexual remark.

"That's good that you have, you can probably give him some private lessons after this adventure," The tour guide joked.

We both laugh and follow him inside the stable to pick out the right horses for our experience.

Finally, picking out the horses, we're showed how to get the horse to slow down, stop, or even speed up. The start of our trip was hot, due to the beaming sun on the way to the beach, once we got to the water, it was so much fun. Just watching Treasure take off in the water on the stallion, it was beautiful. Deciding that we would race for a certain distance, made it even more fun. I end up falling off the horse, not being able to slow him down. Making it to the end of the tour, which lasted for about 2 hours. We decide to go to Blue Beat Ultra Lounge to enjoy some music, eat and chill for the night.

* * *

Arriving at the lounge, we find some sets upstairs on the balcony with the view of the ocean and sunset in perfect view. I order me a Corona and Treasure order's a Martini. Deciding to get something to eat as well, we both end up getting a lobster meal. The best thing about being here on the island the seafood was fresh. Everything was cooked perfect and prepared upon requests and not just sitting out.

"I love the food; it's just so fresh and divine, everything I have eaten since being here has this unique taste to it," Treasure says.

"Yes, it does, I must ask to see what spices they use in their lobsters?" I respond.

After eating our meal, we order one more drink and decided to dance and enjoy the vibe for the rest of the night.

We make it back to the resort, shower, and call it a night.

Day Five

Last Day In Jamaica

Today is our last day in Jamaica. I didn't plan anything extravagant for the daytime. Just for us to go out on seven miles and enjoy the sunset for the evening. The view was beautiful, and we walked, under along the shore, and talked about everything. It wasn't until we got back to the resort and there I had dinner planned outside on the beach. To my surprise, it was a party going on as well. We set out at the resort enjoying are meal together, talking about the time we spent together. Deciding to dance along to the music that was playing under the stars, we do just that. Moving and grooving to the music and laughing enjoying the moment, it wasn't until this drunk guy pushed Treasure and me the gentlemen that I am, I tap him on his shoulder and asks him to apologize because he knocked her over. This man just didn't know who he was talking to; he responded with, "The bitch needs to watch where she going, and I wouldn't have knocked her over," The drunk yelled. Before, I could even think I punched him and kept going until I saw blood. Shoving everybody near me away from me. I walk off and still filled with anger, and not knowing how to calm myself; I just lay under the stars. Lost in my thoughts and not knowing how to calm myself.

Sitting up and noticing Treasure walking towards me in tears, she walks up to me, and instantly goes off, "You didn't have to do him like that," she yells.

"Shut up, stop talking to me you don't tell me how to react when it comes to defending you," I say.

"Now what if he press charges, what are you going to do then," She says.

"Don't worry about it, now leave me alone matter of fact lets go in the room," I say.

She storms off ahead of me, crying hysterically.

Grabbing my head, I realize I have fucked up. I scream out of anger, not knowing what to do next.

Catching her before she can make it to the room, I grab her hand, and she pulls away from me.

"Treasure, please don't do this to me. I'm sorry he took me out of character," I say.

Making it into the room, she turns towards me with bright red eyes due to her crying so much, and yells, "Leave me alone, I no longer know you," She storms into the bathroom and slams the door.

115

Trying to walk in with her, but she locks the door behind her instantly.

"Open the door, I'm sorry, let me show you I'm sorry," I yell.

"Go away, Davion, leave me alone," she says, turning on the shower.

"Please open, the door Treasure I'm sorry,

Realizing that she's not giving in, I leave the room and go sit in the lobby and order me a few drinks and try to call Darren. With no answer, I just ordered more drinks and stayed out of the room until it was time to go.

Not having much sleep last night, I go to the room and pack my luggage. Not even wanting to take a shower due to me still being upset about last night's events. I wait for Treasure to come out of the room, and we check out. I put my shades on and grab luggage, and we walk to the waiting cab. The plane ride home, she still wouldn't say anything to me, so I drift off to sleep.

Waking up right before we land, and looking over to her next to me sleep, I kiss her cheek and reaches for her hand. She wakes up and pulls her hand away from me in a hurry. Counting to myself, because I see now she is very stubborn, and this is not going to be easy. We have gotten to close for me to give up, and that's not an option for me.

Upon exiting the plane, we take the rental I ordered, and head home. I try to explain to her that I have anger issues, but it only comes out when I have to protect those who I care about. With no progress, she tunes me out, and I notice a tear fall from her face underneath the shades she had on.

Arriving to her house, I help her even though she wasn't talking to me. I drop her luggage off in front of her door, and before walking away. I tell her I'm sorry once again. I refuse to let her get away from me due to my range. I had to convince her I didn't mean to shove her or even react the way I did to the drunk stranger. I instantly send her a gift to her job with a card that says I'm sorry, please don't leave me.

Ten

After the Trip

Treasure

Getting home after leaving Jamaica was a relief. I can't believe me and Dave had our first confrontation. He won't be hearing from me after that little scene he caused. I didn't know what to do; next, it all caught me off guard, and so unexpectedly. Placing his calls and texts on mute, continuing with my life as if we never crossed paths. To my surprise, this man doesn't give in. Arriving at work Monday morning, and making my way upstairs to my office. Soon as I open my office door, there is a banquet of roses sitting on my desk, a jewelry box, and card. I toss both items in my bottom file cabinet and put the flowers in the window.

Checking to make sure I have my birth control pills with me to take them, I realize for the past two months, I haven't taken them. Panicking because, during the trip, Dave hasn't used a condom, and me being so caught up in the moment didn't bother to make him. "Fuck, Fuck, Fuck, how could I be so stupid," talking to no one in particular. Crying in silence to myself, realizing if I am, there is only one option left to. I refuse to have another man's child without him being there to help me support him/her. Trying to gather myself so I can start my work. I send Starr texts to see how she is doing and to see if she would come over this weekend her and Trinity. I need some comfort and someone to talk to before I go with my first mind if I am.

Making it through the day with ease avoiding to leave my office for the rest of the week. I would either bring me something from home for lunch or just order something from nearby. Shutting everything out, but making it to work daily all this week is gone be the hard part. My mind is just swarming with so many thoughts of doubts. Like it's crazy how you can be on cloud nine with someone and just one wrong move can make you distances yourself quickness. I know this dark cloud of anxiety and depression was really about to kick me in the ass.

Trying to make it through the weekend without even thinking about it. I even avoid meeting up with Starr during are lunch

break, because I was just confused on what my next move is. I just wanted to be to myself so I can figure things out on my own. The advice Starr gives I can use that as guide on what to do, with a clear mind.

The weekend gets here and Starr shows up, as expected. She never responded to my text but she did make her way to visit me. Trinity rush through the door and yells "Treasure we're hear, where are you." Just hearing her voice changes my mood instantly, Thinking about my little girl, I really need to figure out away to tell Dave about her.

"Hey there lady, I'm sorry I didn't respond to you when you texted," Starr says.

"It's fine you're here that's all that matter really matter," I assure her.

"So what's been going on, I haven't saw you since you left. How was the trip to begin with did something go wrong because you have went back to your old self again and I don't like, Starr says.

Going to get my iPad for Trinity to play with, and getting a glass of wine for Starr, "Give me a second its gone be a long story," I say. "Okay, I have the time, I'm all ears," She say.

"Oh, boy where do I begin?" I ask.

"Begin with the trip in general what did yawl do, what places did yawl visit?" Starr says.

"Alright, I will start from the beginning and let you know what caused this dark cloud," I reply.

Reminiscing on the trip, well it started out great. Our first day there was perfect, we spent the first few hours making love. In to my surprise, he had a romantic spa date setup for us. We enjoyed every bit of it. It wasn't just a body massage it was a relaxing bath together spa date, with a full body massage. We spent the first day inside, enjoying each other company. The few days ahead we had so much fun. We went to visit Dunn's river fall and took some pictures the view was beautiful and after that we went swimming with dolphin's. Like the entire time there I had a smile on my face daily. Every night we had sex and every time it was enjoying, we played sex games, role played.

Everyday we went out to explore something different, it wasn't until are last night there that this other side of him came out. It started because this guy, bumped into me and refused to say excuse me. He went crazy, and I tried my best to get him to calm down and nothing worked. He beat the dude so bad I was scared that the guy would have press charges on him. I know it was all in defense but somethings can be overlooked and ignored. We get to the room and girl he goes to eat me out and whispers so many times how sorry he was.

* * *

It made me flash back to when Trenell would get violent with me and try to have sex with me right after slapping me senseless. I didn't like that side of him at all. It's like everything I said to him after getting him to stop beating the guy was coming in one ear and out the other. He actually shoved me into the wall, when he did stop beating the guy. That took the cake for me right there I ignored him for the rest of the trip. He left the room and didn't return until it was time to check out, after trying to get my attention and it didn't work.

"Wow, damn that's crazy, he was wrong for putting his hands on you. Do I need to go take a trip to visit him?" Starr asks.

"It's okay he has been sending gifts consistently all this week," I respond.

"Awe he is trying to apologize, I think he was so upset and you trying to stop him had him caught up in a rage," Starr says.

"If you don't go get your man before you miss your beat. I will personally bring him to you myself and I have the key so you gone come home from work one day and find him half naked in a apron cooking in the kitchen, waiting on you to come home," Starr chuckles and say to me with this look of seriousness in her face.

"I got something else to tell you, but I'm not sure don't say anything.

I maybe pregnant," I hold my head down and say to her.

"What oh my god, how I thought you was on the pill," Starr says.

Reaching in my purse tossing her my pills she opens them and shakes her head.

"So what are you going to do, and you know if you is you have to really find the time to tell him about Chasity, someway," Starr says.

Looking at Starr and tears run down my face, because I really don't know how he would react and if I want to go along with the pregnancy if I am. She reaches over and hold me.

"Now you know if you need my help with any of it, I'm here for you," She say.

She picks up some Kleenex and hands it to me.

"Stop crying, we gone get through this together both situations if you are," Starr assures me.

"Alright, thank you for coming over. I appreciate it a lot," I say.

"So, speaking of little Miss Chasity when do you plan on starting the visitations after her birthday," She asks.

"Yes, I just don't know what to do or how to go about honestly if I am," I say.

"Please stop don't worry yourself about it because things are going a little left field for you and Dave please," Starr says.

"Okay, I will, Is yawl hungry?" I ask.

"Yes, lets cook something together, lets do steak tacos," Starr suggest.

"Okay, we just have to go to the grocery store to get a few things," I say.

Leaving out the house and taking Starr's car we all get in, and make are way to Jewels. Pulling up in the parking lot of Jewel's we get out and go shopping for our steak taco dinner. Glad to be able to clear my head spending time with my bestie and God-daughter for the weekend will get me out of my zone. Making it back to my house we start cooking, and I go run Trinity a nice warm bubble bath. Starr turns on my music from my sound bar, and pour herself a glass of wine. She goes into my room to find herself something comfortable to put on after she take her shower. "Don't put on my new PJ's I know you like to take all my good shit,"

I yell.

"Okay, I won't," she says while laughing.

Talking to Trinity, "Your mama gone make me have to hide my clothes," I say.

"Yeah she is," Trinity responds.

Letting her play in the tub for a little while I go check on the Steak. Going past my guest room Starr is laying across the bed on the phone with this Kool-Aid grin plastered across her face.

I know instantly who she is talking to so I yell, "Tell Darren I said hey." "Darren, Treasure say to tell you hi," She says.

"He say call his brother that man tripping and going through it,"

She yells'

"I will think about it," I respond.

Not really trying to hear anything he have to say I ignore Darren and go finish tending to my God-daughter.

Starr comes out the room and goes to finish cooking. I go get in the shower after getting Trinity ready.

I get out the shower and Starr has fixed Trinity plate already. "So the food is done?" I ask.

"Yes, indeed it is girl, I'm about to go take my shower and eat when I get out," Starr says.

"Okay, I will wait on you than, I will find a movie to watch," I say. Ten minutes pass and I find a good movie we could all sit and enjoy.

Starr comes out the bathroom with my new pajamas on anyway. Shaking my head because I just knew she wasn't gone listen.

Making my way to the kitchen to fix my plate, she walks in behind me.

"Girl these pajamas are cute where did you get these from?" She asks.

"Oh those I picked up while in Jamaica, Dave actually picked them out," I respond dryly.

Starr goes to fix her plate of tacos, and rice. We both find a spot and got comfortable on the couch and chilled for the rest of the night.

Eleven

Missing Chemistry

Dave

What a roller coaster full of fun we been having. I'm talking from trips and nights of love making we spent with each other.

Her ass was a freak had my dick hard every time I was around her. I never even bothered to be sure if she was on birth control, but I always made sure I strapped up. If I could recall our last trip, I don't think I used any of the magnums I bought. I had to go check my luggage to be sure I wasn't tweaking. I open my bag and true enough a whole box of condoms still sealed. After two weeks of not hearing from her I take matters into my own hands. Deciding to play it safe, I said to myself don't jump to conclusions. I'm just gone wait tell she bring it to my attention, but if she is, we got to change somethings. I need my woman to be in my presence if she is carrying my child. So, before I could find out if she is or not, I decide head over to her apartment leasing office to find out how long she has on her lease and drop a payment for the remainder months left. Letting the manger know before leaving to not to take any further payments from her just deposit it back into her account. After, I did that, I decided to see if she was home and to take her out. To my surprise she was home. I walk up to her doorstep and ring her bell.

"Coming just a second,"she yells.

It takes her a minute to come open the door. She opens the door and something about her makes me smile from ear to ear.

" I haven't been feeling well so I took the day off," she says.

"You must be reading my mind because that was the first

thing I was going to ask. So, do you feel up to part to go out for lunch?" I ask. Scratching her head, "Sure why not where to? I really don't have a specific place in mind." She responds.

"That's fine with me lets do something light," I suggest. We decide to take my car and to go to Panera bread down the street from her house. As we enter Panera bread, she grabs my hand something she had a habit of doing while in public. I can't lie a nigga felt good to have a woman who loved to be seen holding hands and showing public affection. We order to dine in, she orders a broccoli bread bowl soup and I order the same just to see what it tastes like. Breaking the silence between us I speak first.

"I'm not upset at you for ignoring my calls or texts. I understand you needed time to adjust. I'm glad you're talking to me, really thought I lost you."

"Oh, did you really think that, because you didn't give up at all, I see," she responded.

I chuckle, her sarcasm and snobby responds is what I love about her. I'm really in for ear full of it after are first fight. I'm just gone setback and let her keep going. The look she was giving me was a look of hurt and disbelief but also happiness. The connection me and this woman has it's scares me because I actually feel a chemistry with someone that is unexplainable. Breaking me from my thoughts she reaches for my hand and just hold it.

* * *

"Where do I begin with this conversation?" She says.

I'm willing to explain and let it all out just bear with me, please." I respond.

She grabs my hand again and reach for my face and looks me eye to eye and say, "If you're not ready to discuss it don't worry about it. It just caught me off guard and made me have to actually go and take a break a minute."

"I understand but in due time I have to tell you about it but since you have told me not to worry about it right now, I will wait." I reply. Sitting back and enjoying our meal, the looks on her face tells me she hasn't quite forgiven me about the incident that happened on the trip. Not really knowing how to get her to forgive me, I decide that I will let her breathe. I was just glad to in her presences even if it was just for a few hours.

Feeling like I may have lost my best friend, I felt lost without her. Evening though we didn't stay together but we did hear from each other daily and spent the weekends with each other all the time. I really don't know how long it will take for her to forgive me for my actions, but I was willing to do anything to get her back. Using the little time to just keep her smiling I do just that.

"So, you know I'm not giving up on us, no time soon, the chemistry between us is like no other." I say to her.

"I hear you," She respond. Hearing her say that let me know that she is still feeling some type of way about the situation. Not trying to make myself upset because she hasn't forgiven me yet, I ask her is she ready to go home. Dropping her off and being myself, I help her out the car, and walk her to the door but before letting her go inside I reach for her face and kiss her passionately. I whisper to her "I love you."

Leaving her with no words to come out her mouth, she walks away without even looking back. I set in my car and my anger takes over. I punch my steering wheel because I can't get mad at her, I should have told her about my rage fits before we got serious. I break down in tears, thinking about all the moments we shared with each other. I don't know how long I set in my car crying before I noticed the very same Silver Malibu parked behind me. I get a quick look at the driver not being able to catch a full glimpse of his face to be sure it was the same guy, he speeds off like a bat out of hell. Shaking me out of my thoughts I make my way home, to see if I can get the plates number from my restaurant recording. I had to find out who the hell was this mysteries person is.

Treasure

I didn't really want to be rude and just slam the door in his face, so I decided to go out with him for lunch. Not really wanting to see him at the moment as of yet, but I suck it up since he showed up at my door unexpected. Letting him know that I need time to breathe but enjoying his presence just change my entire mood. I no longer felt like I was alone or that the dark cloud was over me, being with him. Me allowing my pride to take over me, I act like everything is alright and that I still don't want to be bother by him. When deep down I really miss him, but I don't want to hurt my own feelings in the mist of things. The behavior he displayed are last night in Jamaica was something out of a movie. It caused me to have flash back to when Trenell use to go off on me out of nowhere. Yes, I still suffer from the past abuse. The whole time we had lunch together he kept me smiling and tried his best to break the sadness he felt amongst us.

* * *

Upon departing he kissed me and gave me that feeling we shared on are first date. Before he released my hand he whispered he love me, and I didn't respond. I walked off with a tears in my eyes not because I didn't believe him. It was because I didn't know how to except it or find myself to be able to love again with ease. Stuck dealing with my emotions and not really sure on how to deal with them. I go inside and fix me some tea and decided I would paint, it usually helped me calm down. Using the rest of my day to relax, I do just that. Before I knew I ended my night on my front room couch.

Twelve

Expectations

~ ❧ ~

Treasure

The same signs I had when finding out I was pregnant with
Chasity starts to come about again. Trying to ignore the signs not wanting
to believe them, it wasn't until after eating lunch at work during my break. I
had ordered a spicy Italian six-inch subway sandwich. Literally just under
two minutes of finishing the sandwich it felt like somebody punched me in
my stomach how fast the food came up. Throwing up every piece of the
sandwich, I try to ignore it and get back to work, but I felt so drained and
tired, I had no choice but to leave early. Rushing to the nearest drugstore to
get a pregnancy test. I really can't believe I let myself get so caught up in the
moment and forgotten to take my damn pills for an entire month. Getting
out my car, I notice a male in all black getting out of Silver Malibu, not trying
to panic I continue to go into the store. Watching my surroundings after
entering the store but the hairs on my arms begins to stand up not feeling
good about the situation. I hurry to go get the test and hurry up out the store.
Mad because I wasn't able to see the face, I pick up my pace and after leaving
the store and rush to get in my car. I speed off with no hesitation.

* * *

Making it home, and rushing to go pee on the stick and anxious to get the results hoping they would show that I'm not. I leave the test in the bathroom and go fix me some tea to calm my jumping nerves. Going back into the
bathroom after five minutes, I pickup the test and it says exactly what I didn't want to see. I was pregnant tears fall down my face instantly.

Deciding I would call and tell Dave in the morning. I really do miss him and he hasn't gave up with sending me gifts every other day. He sent me a morning texts like always and started to send good night texts as well. I realized he was not giving up and its only right that I tell him that I am expecting his child regardless of my decision. Going to bed early due to me not feeling so good about the situation. While crying I drift off to sleep with ease.

Dave

It has been over a week and I still haven't heard from Treasure. She left me sitting in my car torn into pieces. That didn't stop me from sending her gifts or texting her everyday and every night. I wanted to show her that I really love her and that I will repair her heart and mean it. Texting her like I do every morning. I text her this morning and literally right after texting her my phone goes off. Hoping it was her and to my surprise it was her, she had respond back to my texts. Smiling I return her message and let her know that I was enlightened to be getting a response from her.

She ends up calling me after that.

"Hey beautiful, how are you?" I ask.

"I'm okay she says, but I need to talk to you in person," She says.

I begin to get paranoid instantly, "Are you okay, is something wrong," I ask.

"Yes, I'm okay I guess, I just need to see you. That's al," She says.

"When would you like to see me?" I ask.

"If you can come now it would be good," She says.

"Okay, I'm on my way," I respond.

Disconnecting and making my way to go get my lady. My mind begins to wonder and instantly, I think about the box of condoms. I smile because she maybe telling me some good news and this will bring us back together after all.

Pulling up to her house, I hope out the car and this big warm feeling comes over me. I ring the door bell and she opens it and embrace me with welcoming arms with tears in her eyes.

She caught me off guard with this sudden change of behavior after giving me the cold shoulder for a while.

"What's wrong, is it something I can fix?" I ask.

She goes into the bathroom and come back with what looks like a used pregnancy test and after looking at, I laugh, "Your not

joking is you?," I say.

She looks at me with her beautiful teary eyes, the last time I saw her face like this was in Jamaica, I wipe her tears and bring her lips to connect with mine, and we share a passionate kiss.

"I'm excited, how do you feel about it?" I ask.

"I'm a emotional mess, it caught me off guard out of nowhere. So right now I'm still bittersweet about it," She says.

"So you know I'm going to be there for you and my baby every doctors appointment, and next to you through the night. I'm not missing out of none of these precious moment," I grab her face looking her directly in the eye and reassuring her she has nothing

to worry about.

"I believe your every word," She responds. Kissing her again and leading her into her room, I take her pants off and fest my way into her love nectar. Whispering to her I'm sorry with every lick and flick of my tongue, I ease my rock hard dick inside of her valley. She was wetter than I expected and I end up getting so lost into the moment I released all of my little swimmers in her. She cries out and cum all over me and whispers she accepts my apology. I couldn't believe it, she will be waddling around carrying my child. Deciding that we would go to the doctor in the morning, to see how far along we we're. I text my boss to let them know I won't be able to make it in tonight due to unexpected emergency. Not wanting to leave her side at all just yet.

Do you have anything to cook in the fridge?", I ask. No response, I get up and she is knocked out. I can't believe it my baby is having our baby. I go into the kitchen to find something to cook for us, I know she probably hasn't ate anything yet by it begin still early in the morning. So, I cook us both a small breakfast, something to put on her stomach. Waking her up so she eats something, she wakes up with this confused worried look on her face. Like she was having a nightmare or something.

I'm sorry I didn't mean to startle you, I had fixed us some breakfast," I say.

Reaching to give her, plate to her, "Oh, thank you can you please bring me a bottle of room temperature water please?" She ask me.

"Sure, but eat something please I don't want you to be hungry," I say.

Going into the kitchen looking in the cabinet I grab her a bottle of water, and bring it to her.

"I'm spending the night with you so we can go to the clinic in the morning," I say to her.

"Okay, that's fine with me," She respond.

Eating a spoon of food and I say after taking like two more spoons, she rushes out of the room.

Throwing up the water and the little food she ate, she starts crying.

I go to in to help her up and wipe her face, "Yes we have to go to the doctor for sure because you can't keep anything down, which is not good," I say.

Helping her back in the room to lay down not really knowing what to do next. I scroll through the television guide to find something on. Finding some action movie to watch, I end up drifting off to sleep.

Waking up because I hear Treasure up throwing again. I get up and go to assist her and she's constantly throwing up.

"I'm about to go to the store to pick you up some soup and ginger ale, you need to keep something down," I say to her.

Running her some bath water before going, I help her in the bath and let her know I will be back. Grabbing her house keys to lock the door behind myself, I go to the store. Picking up her a few cans of soup that should last for few days until we can get some medicine to help her keep her food down. I get myself some frozen pizza, even though I had a taste for some steak I don't want to eat something she may want, knowing our little bug won't allow her to keep it down. Smiling from ear to ear just thinking about the fact that I'm going to be father soon. The thought was like music to my ears. I stop by Wal-Mart on my way back to the house to get me something to sleep in. Just to think in a just about a few months from now I would have a baby seat in the back of my car, empty or with child sometimes. I can't believe it, this gone be my first child. Turning on the music and making my way back to the house, and Treasure is still in the tub.

Going straight to the bathroom to see if she is alright, "Is you feeling okay, I got you soup and ginger ale and saltine crackers," I say to her.

"Okay, thank you, I appreciate it," She say.

Wanting her to get out of bed I straightening up her room, and fix the front room to make it comfortable for her to watch movies on the couch.

Since, I was hungry I decide to put my Di'gorino's pizza in the oven and put her soup in the microwave. Waiting on her to get out the bath, I scroll through Netflix to find something we could both enjoy. She finally gets out, "Oh I see you straightening up my room for me thank you," She says. Going into the kitchen because she smells food and she instantly says, "I'm hungry."

"Oh I have a frozen pizza in the oven, and I heated you up some soup it's in the microwave. I'm about to get in the shower, could you keep a eye on the pizza?" I ask.

"Yes, I can don't be upset if I cut me slice, I think I can eat some without throwing it up," She says.

Getting in the shower for about twenty minutes, I put on my pajamas I had bought and came to chill with her on the couch.

"So you wasn't playing about cutting you a slice I see," I say to her.

"Nope, not at all. It's very good or I just maybe really hungry after all," She says.

Cutting myself a slice and chilling on the couch we find a movie and end up drifting off to sleep.

Thirteen

A New Day

Getting up and getting ready to go check up on our little bug. She get up and take care of her morning hygiene like always and go straight to the kitchen right after. She goes to make her a cup of tea, her morning routine. She goes to find something comfortable to wear to the doctor. I just setback and let her do her morning activity. I realize she is a person that does things routinely everyday, I had to break her out of that because she may not know if its somebody watching her and knows her every move especially when it comes to traveling.

I go get ready for the day, with ease. After we have both gotten ready we make are way to the doctor's office. Off to the doctor's office we go to start prenatal care. Tailing behind us in the distance the very same Silver Malibu, neither of us noticing it though. Arriving to the office in good timing, we make are way into the building. Still not realizing the Silver Malibu behind them. The driver speeds off and heads forward with traffic and not wanting them to catch on that he has been following them.

* * *

We sit in the waiting room for about thirty minutes, not realizing this visit would be the longest by it being are first visit for prenatal care. Blood work was done and some of the problems Treasure was having as far as

keeping food was addressed as well. Being prescribed medication to help her from throwing up her food all the time and her prenatal pills as well. The last part we had to complete before leaving was to see

how far along she was. The part I have been waiting for to see how far along we are. Treasure lays on the table and the ultrasound technician closes the door and get to work. Asking her a few questions the usual procedure, and right to take pictures of everything.

"Just to confirm you are ten weeks pregnant, Congratulations. I will print out a few pictures for you guys," The technician says.

Treasure looks at me and she starts crying, I get up out the chair and help her sit up.

"I'm here for you and our child every step of the way she will not be alone during this pregnancy at all," I assure her and pass her some tissue to clean her face.

Leaving the clinic we decide that we would go out to eat and celebrate, the good news. Treasure dose off to sleep as soon as we get in the car to leave. I smile because my baby is tired after having a long day in the doctors office.

Pulling out of the parking lot I notice a the very same silver Malibu that speed off from in front of her house the last day we saw each other. Eyeing the driver through my review mirror making sure he is not following us, he turns down the block. Making it to a stop sign, the damn fool comes out of nowhere and damn near side swapping the passenger side of my car. Swerving over to avoid, hitting the car in front of me, thinking to myself this motherfucker has lost his damn mind.

Treasure wakes up to sound of screeching tires an screams, this loud dramatic scream. Looking at the driver she's realizes its her crazy ex, he had been following her for a while now and she wasn't sure if it was him. He pick the wrong time to want to pop up her in life. "Hold on," I yell. Bracing my hand in front of her and to make a left turn because this fool was trying to hurt the both of us. I pull over immediately, "Is you okay, do you have a clue of who this is. I have notice this vehicle in a lot of places lately," I turn to give Treasure eye contact.

With tears following she responds, "It look like my ex Trenell," She says and holds her head down in disbelief.

I reach for her chin, "You don't have to feel ashamed, you didn't do anything wrong. I will say this though but I

don't play when it comes to someone trying to hurt what's mine, and people I love. If he think he it's okay to go on with this random attacks to try to harm you and my child, he will for sure die on my hands," I say.

"I'm not defending him and anyway at all, trust me if I knew he was out and trying to attack me I would have never even let myself get close to you," She says.

"Well since I know this fool is out and trying to harm you, I will not be allowing you to leave you home alone," I say.

The rage in me starts to build up, I had to let her know, "If this lunatic think he will get away this little rampage or even try to get close to you again, I will be sure to deal with him," I say.

Trying to calm my nerves I reach over and rub Treasures belly to help me calm down and she assists me. Counting to myself in my head before pulling off to get home. Treasure sits in the passenger seat looking even more confused and I don't why, but I was going to find out soon.

"Are you okay for sure?" I ask.

Yes, I am okay, I'm just trying to figure out how long he have been following me and when did he get out," She says.

"It doesn't matter, I don't need you stressing about anything. Just know that we will be going to the gun range soon. Let's go celebrate to bringing more happiness in are life. I will not allow this coward ass nigga to destroy us," I assure her.

"Can we just do something in the house, I don't want to go out tonight just us two celebrate at home," Treasure insists.

"Sure love whatever it is you want to do, let's stop by the grocery store to get a few items and we can go to our house," I say.

"Our place don't you mean your place," Treasure say.

"No, I mean what I said our home. You will not be staying by yourself anymore not with that damn psycho out, especially not while your carrying our child, not in this ballpark you won't," I say while reaching for her hand and kissing it.

"Okay, Mister I like how you jump right into decision making, but I can't leave my house like that,"She say.

"It's okay, I got you don't worry about it," I say tell her.

Making it to the grocery store, I reach over to the glove department and get my gun and place it in my holster on my hip for protection.

Treasure looks at my with this look of surprise and licks he lips, "Oh you're a bad boy and disguise I see, I knew it was in you," She say.

Laughing and waiting for me to help her out the car.

"Come on lady, let's go, " I say while reaching for her hand.

Heading into the grocery store Treasure starts picking up items she would want to eat.

"So, is we cooking dinner together, or is doing all the work?" I ask her.

"Great suggestion it will be fun so let's make dinner together, I be the assistant and you take over," Treasure say.

Grabbing her from behind and kissing her neck I whisper, "Okay, it's a deal as long as I can have you for dessert," I smile and slaps her ass and grab a can of whip cream.

"See that's how we end up with this little bundle of joy now you can't keep your hands off me," Treasure laughs can't help it, I love to give my woman attention so she have no reason to seek it elsewhere," I say.

"I love every bit of it especially the public affection," Treasure say.

Continuing our little grocery shopping date and preparing for a celebration of our little gift of joy that will complete us and give us a stronger connection. Leaving the grocery store and arriving to what is now our home. I bring all the bags inside and help her get comfortable.

She walks into the kitchen and she just stares off into the space and say,

"I have something to tell you, before we continue with our happy life," She blurts out.

"What is it, that you have to tell me?" I ask.

"Can you wait until after we prepare dinner?" She ask.

"You want a honest answer, no I can't, the thought of knowing you have something to tell me will bother me," I say.

"Okay, well this child won't be my only child," she blurts out.

"Wait what do you mean?" I ask.

"I lied and told Trenell I had an abortion because I didn't want to have anything to do with him. I gave her up for temporary adoption instead," she says.

"What, why come you haven't mention this to me before?" I ask.

"I didn't know how to let you know," she says while bursting in tears.

"So your telling me this man is after you because he think you killed his child?" I respond.

"I-I-I-I-I she stutters, "I'm not sure if that's the reason he is after me or what?" She says.

Not really knowing how to react to Treasure telling me this I walk out the house.

* * *

To Be Continue...

About the Author

T. Heartless (Tami) born and raised in Chicago, IL. New to the writing industry but has been writing since the age of nine. As a child reading, and writing poetry, and short stories was a hobby for her. Tami (T. Heartless) didn't take writing serious until a professor from college gave an assignment during speaking class. She recited a few of her poetry pieces as an assignment. During that time the professor advised her to publish her work and to enter some poetry contests. Taking the advice given she did for a few months, but gave up on it due to life situations. While, pursuing her Bachelor's Degree during a English course while studying at National Louis University, a writing assignment was given. To do a interview biography on someone you know. Choosing to write a short biography about her grandfather and grandmother titled Charles and Pearl: A story of love. The professor admired the story and wanted to publish her story in a magazine called Mosaic. With this 1st publication of her work she decided to take her writing journey a little more serious. Receiving 2nd place in the University Literature magazine Mosaic this gave her the motivation to keep going. Using her life to help her create her own stories. T. Heartless plans to take her skills to the next level in the writing industry to have work in all genres. Taking her time as a mother, and a full-time worker she wants to show her children that reaching their dreams is possible with faith, determination and motivation. A writer of all genres with spoken words to be heard. Be on the lookout for more of T. Heartless projects coming soon. Join her reading support group on Facebook at Heartless Da Writer Presents. Be on the lookout for Dave & Treasure A

Chicago Love Story Part II and Blind By His Toxic Love.

CPSIA information can be obtained
at www.ICGtesting.com
Printed in the USA
LVHW031726241220
675096LV00004B/473